D0871100

There I Shall Be

Home Is Kentucky

Mark Mattmiller

There I Shall Be
Copyright ©2014
by Mark Mattmiller

For information, address Cloud 9 Press,
PO Box 385, Lexington, KY 40588.
ISBN: 978-0-9647286-8-8

Cover and illustrations by Chris Epling
Interior design and layout by Chip Holtzhauer

Cloud **9** Press

For My Grandchildren:

Brannan Catherine, Frances Alexis, Katherine Marie,
Hailey Grace, Parker LeBus, Emerson Grant, Dason
Brooks, Elizabeth Paige, Sara Ella, and Evelyn Greta

"And at home by the fire, whenever you look up, there I shall be— and whenever I look up, there will be you.

Thomas Hardy, _Far from the Madding Crowd_

Contents

Introduction

The inner bluegrass expanse of Kentucky is known for its beautiful farmland. The gently rolling fields are of the most productive loamy soil, the farms are large, and their owners quite prosperous.

A distinct change in the features of the landscape cannot be missed when one travels north, east, or south out of Central Kentucky. The flat land gives way to the hilly terrain, and the loamy soil becomes primarily red clay. This outer bluegrass area is unique in its geography. Flat land for crop production is limited to ridge tops and narrow creek bottoms. The farms are much smaller than the estates of the inner bluegrass. These features - the hills, the clay, and the small size of the farms - have defined the lifestyles and the very personalities of the people who settled and still live there.

To survive, the farmers of the area began raising an acre or two of tobacco as a cash crop. The production of tobacco is extremely labor intensive, and it became necessary for the survival of everyone that equipment and labor be shared. Close tight-made little communities followed.

"There I Shall Be" is a collection of seven short stories stitched together in an effort to capture the soul of this rural life. A kinship has developed that not only follows along the lines of blood relations but is also tied to property ownership as well. The cool and quirky characters are all here. Their bonding, and the commensurate love, tears, and laughs that accompany it, are brought forth in this work.

Chandler Holmes

Ziegler's Branch divided the farms of Jake Barnes and Chandler Holmes. The little creek served as the boundary line between the two properties and created a deep hollow separating Barnes's productive ridge and Holmes's marginal pasture land. The drop from Jake's place to the creek was particularly steep, and in some places it had the look of a small cliff or precipice. The hillside on the Holmes place was not as bad, and there was an old road and footpath from top to bottom. There was no fence along the creek at the bottom of the hillsides, and there never had been. Both farms were fenced along the ridges at the top where the wooded slopes gave way to land that was more level and functional.

The steep slopes of Jake Barnes' farm faced north and were dark and shadowy. Huge cedars mixed with red oaks and hickories were thick. Many of the smaller cedars were leaning or had fallen down; they couldn't compete with the hardwoods for sunlight and were systematically dying. Walking was almost impossible. Ancient shallow gullies, the result of erosion, ran down the slopes every hundred feet or so. These ravines were healed over with moss, ferns, and tree roots. The southern facing slopes on the Holmes farm were not as thickly populated with trees, but the ash, walnuts, and oaks there were larger. The cedars were mostly gone. There were no pronounced gullies here, and the walking was relatively easy.

The creek and the hillsides between the two farms made up somewhat of a no man's land. There was an old logging road that passed through the hollow, and access to the road was easy at the lower reaches of the creek. The area was visited occasionally by the local hunter, the student of nature, or a family on a picnic. It was understood that the property of one was open to the other. Neighbors moved freely from farm to farm. Tools were borrowed, ponds fished, and squirrels hunted. Permission had been granted years in the past, and that was understood. The unspoken, but universally understood, rule was that before entering another's property or shortly thereafter, the owner was to be notified. The land of others was treated with ultimate respect, and the benefit was the extra pair of eyes that would spot and report anything that looked out of the way.

On this particular autumn day, Jake Barnes had entered the old logging road where the creek met his small tobacco bottom. He was on his old Massey Ferguson tractor and was enjoying the slow and pleasant journey up the creek to the deep hollow. He had hitched a carry-all to his little tractor. His mission was to gather a few flat rocks out of the creek bed and use them to fill in a muddy place on the driveway that circled his barn.

Jake knew exactly where in the bed of the stream he was most likely to find the appropriate thin rocks. He backed the tractor down to the edge of the water, lowered the carry-all, and with a pick, he loosened the rocks he needed. The work of loading the stones was not particularly strenuous, but even so, the effort had left Jake a little thirsty. There was an ancient spring on the Holmes side of the small stream, and Jake reckoned that on his way out he'd stop there to quench his thirst. No one really knew who had built the rocked in reservoir and stone enclosure at the cold water spring. It was surmised that a family named Ziegler, who were believed to be the original settlers of that particular farmland, had built it and used it. The earliest settlers always built their log or stone homes close to a dependable source of pure water. Locating the spring, or vein as it was sometimes called, came first, and then the house was built nearby.

An old dirt roadway and easy footpath traversed the hill from the spring up to Chandler Holmes's house, and for decades the previous residents of the old place had made the daily trip down the hillside and then back up. Every drop of the water they needed for cooking, cleaning, bathing, and drinking was carried from the spring to the home in buckets. Before Holmes bought the old homestead, a previous owner had built a cistern at the back door of the house, and that became the primary source of water, but during the droughts of summer when there was no rainwater to fill the cistern, the spring became the back-up source. On washdays and sometimes just to conserve what was in the cistern, Holmes would hitch a feed sled loaded with two wooden barrels to his old tractor and make the trip to the spring for extra water.

For years, Chandler Holmes had kept an old cut gourd hanging at the spring to use as a dipper to drink the cool water. It was not unusual for Chandler to be at the spring in the course of his hunting, foraging, and wood cutting. When it was unusually hot, Holmes would take off his hat, fill the gourd, and pour the cold water over his head. Then he would drink and rest. The place offered the perfect respite from heat and thirst. The gourds were good for only a year or so before they cracked or broke, and Chandler would have to replace them frequently. In a gesture that Chandler Holmes considered to be outrageously extravagant, his wife, Louise, used some egg money to buy a new white and red speckled enameled dipper. Holmes fussed, fumed, and fussed some more about spending the money, but of course, the new dipper made it to the spring.

When Jake Barnes stopped at the spring, he was surprised to find that the enameled dipper was gone. It had hung in the same place for years. After he cupped his hands to drink and splash a little cool water on his face, he took a few seconds to reflect upon the spring and the dipper. Jake mused that the dipper had become an important feature to the setting. It was the only man-made thing in a world of undisturbed nature. Jake wondered how many people over the years drank from the spring; had used the dipper. He couldn't imagine why it was gone. The missing dipper left Jake with a slight sense of uneasiness. It was then that he decided to walk up the hill and visit with his old neighbor.

ooooo◆ooooo

The ninety acre farm of Chandler Holmes was not fertile. The hillsides were poor, and the ridges were marginally productive. The abusive practices of earlier owners had left the soil thin and rocky. The rich topsoil and humus that made up the forest floor before the land was cleared were long gone. Erosion left only a thin layer of red clay. It was teasingly said that a jack-rabbit would have to pack his lunch if he were to pass through the old place.

Holmes had lived on the poor farm with his wife, Louise, since right after World War II. He had bought the land, one barn, and house at a Master Commissioners sale after the previous owners packed up and left for California. When the couple moved in, they were sure their lives would evolve into lives of plenty, but in time, harsh reality dimmed those dreams.

The old farm could produce just about enough to take care of itself and very little else. Like every other farmer in the county, Chandler Holmes subscribed to the practice of going to the bank each year and borrowing enough to live for the next year and to get his one or two acre tobacco crop raised. For the entire year, almost all purchases were made on credit. The grocery and drug stores, the feed store and hardware, the doctor and dentist, all sent one bill annually. When the crop was sold, the bank got theirs first, and the remainder went to all the creditors. For Holmes, there was very little left. Then it was back to the bank to make the arrangements for the next year. A cycle of frugality followed.

The farm drained off whatever money the Holmes put aside to try to break the cycle. Periodically something unforeseen would inevitably come up: the tractor needed repair, fence had to be replaced, a new chainsaw was required, or the barn had to be repaired. They could never get ahead, but the couple did manage to get by. There was not enough income to make adjustments to the budget, so Chandler and Louise Holmes learned over time to adjust how

they perceived their needs. They learned to find happiness not in their possessions but rather in their sense of independence, their ability to provide for themselves, and their support and assistance to each other.

The couple worked together to make every penny count, and they labored together with whatever chores the subsistence farm life required. Most everything the couple needed to survive was provided by their labor and by the farm. Wood was cut to warm the home and fuel the cook stove. Vegetables from the garden and fruit from the pear, plum, and apple trees that grew behind the house were consumed in season and canned for later use. The hen house provided eggs and an occasional roasting hen, and the smoke house was filled late every fall with salted and cured pork from meat hogs that were raised on the place. Chandler Holmes would forage and trap in the woods and hunt the squirrels, rabbits, and quail. They planned their days and their labors together. The hard work became its own reward, and the couple became bound to each other with an undying devotion.

When Louise and Chandler Holmes were in their fiftieth year of marriage, Louise passed away. Chandler Holmes carried on with the cattle and tobacco the best he could without his companion and his soul mate, but the demands of working alone and the stress of living alone at his advanced age soon took its toll. Before long his farming was reduced to some chickens, an old cow, a few hogs, and a rough garden.

The old man had no family that he could lean on or move in with. Old friends dropped in on Holmes periodically to make sure he was well and to see that he had what he needed. Neighbors were there to provide whatever extra help that Holmes might need with his meager farming. He was becoming a cause for concern within the entire community.

Tragically, within the first year after Louise's passing, Chandler Holmes began to show increasing signs of some serious dementia. It became clear to the community that Chandler should be visited almost daily, and a coordinated effort was initiated at the church to make sure that someone checked on the old man. Chandler Holmes deteriorated quickly. He mostly just sat in his rocking chair on his front porch. For years Candler and his wife had sat on the porch in the evenings, and they always waved to the occasional car that would pass by. But the old man no longer waved: he just sat there.

Visitors became particularly alarmed when they

realized that Holmes began to believe that his wife was still living. When the neighbors came to check on him, Chandler would explain that Louise was in town at the bank or was off visiting her sister in Ohio. He usually added that she would be home before nightfall. No one had the heart to tell the old man that she was gone. They just went along with it the best they could.

Soon the discussions at the store and the churches became serious regarding Chandler Holmes. It was becoming apparent that he'd have to be committed, or somebody would have to take him in. Certainly no one really wanted to face the prospect of addressing that with Holmes.

ooooo◆ooooo

Jake Barnes easily found the old pathway that would take him to Chandler Holmes's place. He was surprised at the amount of tree seedlings, briars, and weeds that were growing in the old road. Jake paused for a few moments, stood still, and gazed up and down the old road. He surmised that it had surely been at least a decade since any effort had been made to keep the old access clear. He reflected on his own place, the flat rocks he had just loaded, and how much labor it takes to keep the old hill farms in good shape. Jake Barnes smiled to himself as he grasped the idea that old age was not only seen in the man but in his farmland as well. He pondered himself and his own farm.

As he again began the walk up the hill, Jake observed the hillsides and noted how much larger the trees and brush had grown since he was last there or had last taken the time to observe. At one time the entire farm had been planted in corn, and the result was horrendous; over two feet of rich topsoil washed to the Mississippi delta. A useless wasteland of clay and rock remained. As Jake looked over the terrain and saw that the erosion was stopped, he felt a sense of satisfaction with his observations and knowledge that nature was healing what man had offended. And Jake knew that each passing day lessened the significance of the old road.

Jake reached the top, straddled and the stepped over the low barbed-wire fence that separated the level ridge from the wooded hillside, and headed across the pasture field. It was just a short walk to the driveway that led to the Holmes house. Just as he got to the drive, Jake was met by a pickup truck. The driver was another neighbor, Ernie Stone, who was also going to check on Chandler Holmes.

Ernie leaned out the window as Jake walked up to the truck and said, "Well, well, who let you out?"

Jake laughed and said, "I was just about to ask you the same thing. You checking on Mr. Holmes?"

Ernie nodded and asked, "What are you doing out here on foot? Is everything all right?"

"Yeah, same as you. I was down in the creek and decided to walk up and check on him myself."

"Well hop in," Ernie Stone said.

Jake walked around to the other side of the truck, got in, and rode the short fifty yards to Chandler Holmes's house.

ooooo ◆ ooooo

When Ernie stopped the truck, they saw that Holmes was sitting somewhat slumped on his porch. They were surprised that the old man didn't get up to meet them. "Must be asleep," Ernie said.

"Yeah," said Jake.

"Chandler!" Ernie half shouted as they approached the porch, but the old man didn't reply.

As the men neared Chandler Holmes's porch, they were both hesitant in their gait. Things didn't seem right. A certain dread crept in. When they reached the porch, they stopped, then froze, and remained motionless.

"Oh dear Lord, and look," added Jake as he pointed

to the floor. There lying between the old man's feet where he had dropped it was the white and red speckled dipper.

The Bullet

Fifth grader Woody Ziegler found the big bullets when he was rooting through the piled up and stored boxes of junk in his Uncle Charles' basement. The bullets were in the bottom of an old dusty dark green wooden box and covered with some wire and rusty steel traps. Woody didn't have any idea what kind of bullets they were. He only knew that they were huge. The bullets were almost four inches long, and Woody figured that since his uncle was a World War II veteran, he must have brought them home from the war. What Woody was sure of was that they were the biggest bullets he had ever seen, and that he could hardly contain his excitement when he thought of showing bullets that big to his friends, Peachy Cornett and Artie Shedd. After giving the matter a few seconds of fleeting thought, Woody slipped one of the bullets into his pocket, headed up the stairs, kissed his aunt goodbye, and bounded out the door. The young man was in no way prone to stealing, and in his mind he was only borrowing the huge bullet. He would return it to the box after he showed it to his two friends.

This was the year 1968, and it was not in any way unusual to run across military stuff; the end of World War II led to a proliferation of military surplus goods. In the cities, there were army surplus stores here and there. Huge government auction sales had dispersed the left-over goods and equipment, and it seemed that every household had army blankets, cots, shipping crates, gun belts, canteens, clothes, or even bullets. Assuredly, the tiny community of Mt. Zion, Kentucky was no exception; surplus clothes and blankets were in everyday use, bookends were made of everything from grenades to binoculars, and canteens were commonly carried to the hay fields. But bullets were rare, and Woody's find fit squarely into a young man's category of "extra cool." To Woody, borrowing the bullet seemed innocent enough, but like so many things, hindsight would show that this was the very moment that a whole load of trouble had its beginning.

It was an early September Saturday, and Woody figured that Artie Shedd would be hanging around his house loafing. It was just after noon, and the Shedds were known for not doing much on weekend afternoons. Woody jogged the two blocks from the back street where his aunt and uncle's house was located to the main road through town where the Shedds lived. When he got to the Shedd home, Woody saw that he had figured correctly; the whole Shedd family was sitting on their front porch.

Woody whistled and signaled for his friend to come out to the front yard, and Artie wasted no time.

When they met in the Shedd's front yard, Woody gestured for Artie to move around to the side of the house. It was there that Woody showed his friend the bullet.

"Oh-my-gosh," Artie half shouted. "Where'd you get it?"

"Uncle Charles's basement. Cool isn't it? Biggest bullet I ever saw."

"Me too. Let's go find Peachy. He's gotta see this."

The boys half walked and half ran the two miles to the edge of town and down the highway to the Cornett's long lane.

The gravel lane ran almost three quarters of a mile down Wells Ridge before the land opened up at the Cornett place and sheriff "Rocky" Stone's farm. The ridge was narrow and dropped off steeply on both sides. The hillsides and what little flat land there was on the ridge were covered with second growth timber right up to the gravel driveway. The hickories, oaks, and walnuts grew tall and straight and made a canopy that kept the driveway in semi shade until the leaves dropped with the coming of winter. Both sides of the road were fenced with rickety and rusty woven wire that was patched here and there with barbed wire. Any fence posts that had been set for the original fence were long gone, and for decades the farmers had given in to the common practice of nailing the old and the new wire to the tree that was closest to the original line. The result was a fence that meandered, and wire that was deeply imbedded into the wood.

The two boys had walked about half way down the driveway when they came upon Walt Cornett who was working alone repairing a bad place in the weak fence. Walt was the father of Peachy, Shorty, and their older sister, Dorothy.

"Hello, Mr. Cornett," both boys said almost in unison.

"Well, well, look what the cat drug in. Woody Ziegler and Artie Shedd. If this isn't an exciting combination. What are you two up to?"

"Looking for Peachy, Mr. Cornett. Is he around?" Woody asked.

"In fact, he's not." Cornett replied. "He's staying at Dorothy's and may or may not be in at all today."

Dorothy was the oldest of the three Cornett siblings and was recently married to John Lewis. What all three of them knew was that when Peachy got the chance to visit his sister, he would become fixated on dreaming up ways to stay as long as he could. John

Lewis was a pleasant and easy going man who was fun to work with. And equally important was the location of his farm on the big bends of the South Fork River. Peachy could fish, forage, and explore on foot or with the john boat. Life at his sister's was relaxing for Peachy: he was mostly left alone to roam the woods and the river banks, and those two places had become the young man's preferred element.

"So if you're not going any further, how about helping me for a few minutes with this fence?" Walt Cornett added.

"Sure," Woody answered while Artie nodded. The boys were well schooled on the importance of helping whoever asked. The young men were also always anxious to demonstrate their manhood and the level of their knowledge of the farm-work world.

When Mr. Cornett walked to his pickup truck to get the boys some work gloves, Artie Shedd whispered to Woody, "Should we show him the bullet? I bet he'd know what kind it is."

"No way!" hissed Woody. "We'd get nothing but about ten thousand questions."

The three men, one old and two young, worked well together. Cornett showed the boys the stretch of about fifty yards of old, rusty, half-gone, and weak woven wire fence that he was replacing with three strands of barbed wire, and the threesome got started. The old fence was to be cut away from the trees with bolt cutters, rolled up into short batches, tramped flat, and carried to a wash-out close by. The trees were skinned with an axe of all bark and left-over wire and staples. Finally the new barbed wire was stretched and stapled to the trees. They spoke very little as they worked, and their labor presented a clear picture of coordination. The movements of one seemed to complement the efforts of the others: the axe was handed over at just the right moment; the single-wire stretcher fastened, the trees marked, and the wire stapled without much more than a nod and with little wasted time or effort. Walt Cornett was not surprised by the young men's knowledge or abilities: most of the boys of Mt. Zion had tools in their hands from the time they were old enough to tag along.

ooooo◆ooooo

Peachy Cornette, Artie Shedd, and Woody Zeigler were viewed to be inseparable. If there was any way possible, the three of them would be together. They were considered to be good boys, and whatever mischief they got into was always along the lines of that old saying about "boys being boys." Woody and Artie were naturally disappointed that they couldn't see Peachy that day and would have to put off showing him the giant bullet. They would have to wait until they met the next morning for their walk to school.

Peachy and Artie were already waiting when Woody showed up at their usual meeting place. Of course Artie had filled him in on the huge bullet, and Peachy's first words to Woody were, "OK, let's see it."

"Yeah, check this out," Woody responded as he handed the bullet to Peachy.

Peachy Cornett was the unnamed leader of this little trio, and it was his opinion that mattered the most, so Woody and Artie broke out in smiles when he said, "Holy Moley, look at that. Extra cool!" Then he added, "What are we going to do with it?"

Woody didn't hesitate when he replied with, "I really should get it back to Uncle Charles' basement."

"Yeah, but what about right now? It might not be too good of an idea to take it into the school," Artie added.

"Yeah, maybe I should hide it before we go in," said Woody.

"Awe, it won't hurt, just keep it in your pocket. We

haven't got time to do anything else right now," said Peachy.

And with that, the three headed down the road to school.

○○○○○◆○○○○○

The three boys were in the sixth grade at the local elementary school. Rock Creek Elementary had been serving the little hamlet of Mt. Zion, Kentucky and the surrounding countryside for generations. There was nothing unusual about the building, the teachers, or the students. They all had their roots in the red clay hill country around Mt. Zion. The farms were hilly, the buildings modest, and the people hard working and mostly honest. There were six classrooms in the old schoolhouse, and they were separated by the long wide hallway typical of the structures of their age. The principal's office was in the center and a small cafeteria at one end. In the basement were the bathrooms and the furnace room.

It was in the furnace room that the boys met every morning to talk and joke a little before the bell rang for class to begin. It was also here in the furnace room, on this particular day, that things went a little haywire.

The janitor for the school was Mr. Claude Savage, and he always had a few hand picked sixth-graders to help him when he needed it. The trio of Peachy, Woody, and Artie were his picks for the year. He didn't mind the boys hanging out in his combination furnace room/office. In fact he enjoyed their company and joined in with their banter and teasing.

It was not unusual for Mr. Savage to leave the boys alone in the furnace room. He would be called upon to perform some repair job, lifting task, plant watering chore, snow shoveling ordeal, or any other miscellaneous errand that came up. On this morning, he was summoned to close a stuck window, and he left in a hurry. As soon as he walked out of the door, Woody pulled the bullet out of his pocket so they could admire it some more.

After they all got another look, Artie and Woody noticed that Peachy Cornett got a certain wild eyed far-away look on his face. The two had seen the look before, and they knew from experience that the next words out of Peachy's mouth would somehow suggest that they do something daring and right on the edge of crazy.

Peachy Cornett didn't disappoint his two companions when he said, "Wonder what would happen if we threw it in the furnace?"

"You're crazy. What do you think would happen? It'd explode!" Woody said.

"Yeah, but if it did, we wouldn't be here. We'd be in class. Wonder how long it'd take?" said Peachy.

"It might not even explode," Artie said. "It might just fizzle."

"You're both crazy. I've got to take the bullet back to Uncle Charles's basement," Woody half shouted. "No way you can talk me into this."

"It might be kinda of fun sitting in the class waiting."

"Yeah, if it did go off, nobody would ever figure out what it was."

"Can you imagine the look on Miss Fennimore's face if it exploded loud enough for us to hear upstairs?" Peachy asked.

"But, but, listen," insisted Woody.

"Awe come-on Woody, let's have a little fun with it. You said there were lots of them at your uncle's. He'll never miss just one," insisted Peachy.

"I'll go guard the door and make sure Savage isn't coming," said Artie.

"Yeah, and here, I'll hold the furnace door open for you," added Peachy.

Woody stopped moving like he was stunned. He stood perfectly still for several seconds. Then he nodded to his companions and watched as Artie moved to the furnace room door, and Peachy lifted the heavy steel handle to the Rock Creek Elementary School furnace.

∞∞∞∞◆∞∞∞∞

The threesomes headed straight to their class the second the bullet was tossed into the furnace and the steel door closed. Of course they were a bit nervous and tried not to let it show: the boys were serious and quiet when they made their entrance into the classroom that morning, and that was certainly a change. Their nervousness and anxiety continued as Mrs. Fennimore went through the regime of starting the day. The teacher checked the class attendance, led the class in prayer, and joined with the students in saying the pledge to the flag.

The three boys didn't sit together in the classroom: even Mrs. Fennimore had enough sense not to let that happen. But they were close enough to each other to be able to make eye contact and use their own particular sign language to communicate when the occasion was right. A cough, a dropped pencil, or a scratched ear had their own secret meanings.

When Mrs. Fennimore had the class start on the daily vocabulary exercise, all three boys were acting like they were attentive, studious, and involved in the lessons. But in reality, all three were operating with a high degree of nervousness as they waited to hear from the bullet. When the vocabulary lesson was completed and nothing had come from the furnace room, the boys were beginning to suspect that the bullet was a dud. The class was halfway through the following math lesson and still nothing. It was about then that the three young men began to send little signals. They relaxed with their resolve that the bullet must have fizzled; nothing was going to happen.

Then it happened. No, no, it wasn't a pop. No, it wasn't a bang. It was huge! **"BALOOM!!"** like a bomb! The room shook. The explosion amplified as it went threw the furnace ducts and came out into the rooms. A significant puff of dust came with the titanic explosion as the vibration shook loose some of the dirt that had accumulated in the vents.

The explosion was followed by about twenty seconds of complete silence. Then Betsy Heimer started crying, and Mrs. Fennimore slowly came out from under her desk: she was white faced, and her hands were shaky. All of the students started jabbering at once. There was complete confusion. A close look would have revealed that Woody Ziegler's eyes were wide as saucers, Artie Shedd had dropped his head to his desk, and Peachy Cornett had the slightest smile.

Mrs. Fennimore then hurried across the room, out the door, and into the hall. Every single teacher in the entire building had done the same thing. They were all talking and shouting back and forth to each other. The scene could have best been described as panicky confusion. It was then that the fire-drill alarm went off and everyone left the building in their practiced routine.

ooooo ◆ ooooo

It took considerable time for Mr. Savage and the principal, Mr. Woodruff, to determine that the building was safe and that it was all right for the students to go back to their classrooms. It was hard for the three boys not to laugh as they made their way up the stairs and into the building. They were feeling downright full of themselves.

Ms. Fennimore was having trouble getting her class to settle down. Betsy Heimer was still sniffling.

The entire class was fidgety and noisy.

Then Mr. Woodruff came through the door; things changed instantly. The school principal was a huge man, and no one, teacher, parent nor student, relished messing with him. On this occasion, he was obviously very driven and tense.

He stood before the class, and there was complete silence. It was then, in a huge and deep voice, that he bellowed, "I know who did it!"

His words staggered Peachy, Woody, and Artie, but they tried to act just as calm as they possibly could.

The principal half shouted, "I know exactly who you are."

And then, "I know who the perpetrator is, and he'd better come forth."

The three boys weren't exactly sure if they'd ever heard the word "perpetrator" before, but on this day they had no doubt what it meant.

When Woodruff again said that the perpetrator had better stand up, Woody and Peachy both noticed that sweat was starting to pop out on Artie Shedd's forehead. The two boys were thinking, *"Oh no, Artie, no."*

"If the perpetrator doesn't come forth, the punishment will be the maximum allowed by the law."

Artie began sweating and turning white all at the same time. *"No, Artie, no,"* Peachy and Woody silently begged.

"I know who you are!" Woodruff roared.

Peachy Cornett and Woody Zeigler figured they were doomed when they noticed that Artie had not only turned white and was sweating profusely, but was beginning to shake all over as well. *"He's bluffing, Artie. Don't cave in. Hang in there."*

Artie Shedds lips began to quiver.

"No, Artie, no!"

"Stand up now, and admit to your crime. **Stand up now**," the principal barked.

That did it. Artie Shedd jumped straight up and shouted, **"I didn't throw no bullet in no stove!"**

Mr. Woodruff very calmly and very slowly questioned, "You didn't throw no bullet in no furnace?"

"No, sir, I was just the lookout'" Artie answered.

Of course everyone in the room had noticed

that Peachy Cornett and Woody Zeigler had both dropped their heads to their desks when Artie let go with his outburst. Mr. Woodruff turned his attention to Peachy and asked, "I guess you didn't throw no bullet in no furnace either?"

"No Sir, I just held the furnace door open."

"Artie, Woody, and Peachy to my office, now!"

That was the day three young men from Mt. Zion Kentucky learned that the degree of involvement mattered not one nit. It was of no significance whatsoever if one was the idea dreamer upper, the looker outer, the door holder opener, or the bullet thrower inner. Involvement is always its own equalizer, consequences uniformly administered.

Perceptions

Some of the students in Mrs. Virginia Ashberry's fourth grade class grimaced when she said it. Some dropped their heads and wouldn't look. Others looked off or just focused on nothing. None were shocked: it wasn't the first time the teacher had humiliated Lawrence Sears in front of the entire class.

"Spit it out," she said, "spit it out!" Mrs. Ashberry had Lawrence standing in front of the class to take his turn at reciting the Robert Frost poem.

"T_,T_, Two, Ro,Ro Roads, Di_,Di_, Di."

"Diverged, Lawrence, diverged. Just say it. We haven't got all day."

Lawrence Sears was a big, timid, very quiet, immature boy with a slight speech impediment that naturally became more pronounced when he was nervous. He was not Virginia Ashberry's favorite student, and she made no bones about it.

ooooo ◆ ooooo

Lawrence Sears was the second son of the community pillar, Karl Sears. The Sears family had always been considered amongst the most prominent in the Mt. Zion area. For generations, they farmed the big bottoms along the South Fork River and lived in relative comfort. Like most of his family, when Karl completed his high school studies, he attended State University in Lexington. In the ensuing five years, Karl earned degrees in math and accounting, married his high school sweetheart, and returned to Mt. Zion to begin his career as a CPA. His business was good from the onset, and like all Sears, Karl had the respect of the community.

Carl and his wife, Anna, were blessed early in their marriage with two sons. First there was LaFayette, called "Faye", and then three years later, Lawrence was born. Both boys were born into lives of privilege and unbounded love, but they demonstrated from early on that they were in fact dissimilar in most all observable ways.

Faye Sears was of medium height and slightly built. Lawrence, on the other hand, was always very tall for his age and muscled up almost from infancy. Where Faye would move quickly and almost catlike, his younger brother seemed always to be in slow motion. When they played together, which was a large part of every day, it was almost as if Lawrence was just an extension of Faye. Faye would plan and direct the course of their activities to such a degree that he was, in fact, doing most of Lawrence's thinking for him.

LaFayette "Faye" Sears was very bright, and from the beginning he excelled at the little elementary school just south of Mt. Zion Kentucky. He quickly became the favorite of all the teachers at Rock Creek Elementary and remained so until he left. Faye got the accolades: he would be assigned the leading roles in school plays, the solos in the little choir, and of course, he was the champion at spelling bees. His grades were always excellent. The young man's confidence was boundless, and it seemed to all that he could excel at everything. Faye Sears could do no wrong, and his future was bright.

Lawrence on he other hand, just eased through his first three years. He was a pleasant child and liked by everyone, but he didn't in any way shine at his schoolwork. His earliest teachers recognized that he was somewhat immature and perhaps not the brightest young student; however, they were for the most part confident that he would grow out of his poor academic performance. Lawrence was not faced with unreasonably lofty expectations.

ooooo◆ooooo

Virginia Ashberry was raised as an only child by a sullen mother and an overbearing father. Her parents were consumed with work and with making money. They worked, saved, spent very little, and worked some more. Theirs was a life of self-imposed misery as they tended to their poor, hilly, red-clay farm. They were suspicious of everybody and stayed mostly to themselves. Laughter, pleasantries, and frills were not in the life of Virginia Ashberry. The young lady had little chance for happiness and no chance whatsoever for developing even a small degree of confidence.

Throughout her youth and young adulthood, Virginia planned for and dreamed of the day that she would get away from the life of her childhood. She was driven to do well in school and continue with her education until she could become a teacher and be on her own. Only then could she live a life with some semblance of normalcy. She imagined herself as ultimately being married and having children that she could raise in a positive and loving setting.

Virginia did, in fact, complete high school, manage to attend the teachers college, graduate, and get a job at the Rock Creek Elementary school. Unfortunately, her plans for bliss didn't materialize: happiness continued to elude Virginia. The young teacher strived for popularity and acceptance with her peers, but her poor self esteem interfered. Gradually misunderstanding became condemnatory, and

Virginia Ashberry slowly drifted towards bitterness. As she approached middle age, each school day became the maker of misery.

When LaFayette Sears was placed in Ms. Ashberry's fourth grade class, he came with the reputation of a bright and dedicated student. But it was in her class that he began to excel beyond anyone's expectations. He started to read the adult classics and quoted from them without hesitation. On his own, he began to study algebra when the rest of the class was struggling with the principles of long division. His self esteem was unbounded: nothing was too challenging for Faye Sears, and soon the entire community was proudly calling him a prodigy.

For teacher Virginia Ashberry, these were the shining moments of her life. She began to believe that it was because of her expertise that the young man was doing so well. Every new success of the young student brought Virginia a commensurate feeling of success and pride. At long last she was feeling positive about herself. She began to imagine that the other teachers were seeing her in a different light and holding her in high regard. The entire experience was exhilarating for Ms. Ashberry. At last she was somebody.

When the school year ended, Virginia was beset by a slow and persistent tailspin. A void was replacing the grand feelings of success. Her newfound self esteem and perceived respect left with Faye Sears. Gloom filled the void, and Virginia was once again slipping into bitterness.

ooooo◆ooooo

The next three years were not good for Virginia Ashberry. She became increasingly more and more sullen. She felt that she was not appreciated by her peers, and began to believe that she was not liked. Her poor self regard began to take over, and her sullenness drifted into anger. The young teacher didn't smile or laugh, and she rarely engaged in conversation. Of course, the school staff did, in fact, begin to avoid Virginia, and soon her days were spent in miserable self imposed social isolation.

When the little brother, Lawrence Sears, enrolled in Miss Ashberry's class, her spirits immediately began to pick up. She was sure that the young man would be equal to his older brother in all regards, and she was equally sure that she would be seen as the reason for his imminent unbounded success. The other teachers and the principal would again recognize Virginia's special ability to bring out the very best in the more gifted students. She fantasized that one more success like she had with Lafayette Sears would bring to her a special status where she would be assigned only the most gifted students. Virginia Ashberry started the school year with a bounce in her step: she was invigorated with anticipation.

When Lawrence Sears entered Virginia Ashberry's class, her expectations for the boy were utterly and totally unreasonable. The teacher expected Lawrence to excel as had his older brother, and that just wasn't going to happen. From the onset, Lawrence's extreme timidity and immaturity were perceived by Miss Ashberry as obstinacy.

Lawrence was never a discipline problem, nor did he ever create any kind of classroom distraction. The young man just daydreamed away the school day. He could make a broken pencil into a car and the desktop into a racetrack as in his mind he recreated the Indianapolis 500. In addition, Lawrence rarely got around to completing his homework. He did not do well in her class. When the teacher began to increase the pressure on Lawrence, he shut down completely. He began to shirk all responsibility for his class work, and in a short time, Miss Ashberry's high expectations for Lawrence and for herself faded into a sense of no hope whatsoever. She began to blame the boy for her own inadequacies and failures. Eventually, she got to where she never missed a chance to single out the poor boy with hatefulness and humiliation. Lawrence's poor performance was the fatal blow to Virginia Ashberry's self esteem. It was not a good year for either of them.

∞∞∞∞◆∞∞∞∞

Life for Virginia Ashberry never improved. After Lawrence Sears left her class to go on to the next grade, she could visualize no hope whatsoever for personal recognition. And to top it off, she no longer had the young student to blame. The emptiness she felt was debilitating. Miss Ashberry rarely smiled. She walked through the school as if she were in a fog. Soon the other teachers began to talk, and that led to avoidance. A few of the older teachers tried to reach out to Virginia, but they were met with rebuff. The principal, who was himself totally inept, did what he always did: he ignored Virginia and the problems she was creating.

Virginia Ashberry left the teaching profession shortly after Lawrence Sears left for the high school. She married an old and wealthy widower, who lived in Hawkinsville, four miles down the highway.

Simon Garr was known as a jolly man, but marriage to Virginia Ashberry took its toll, and it wasn't long before the two of them were being referred to as the "no smilers." The old schoolteacher withdrew completely and lost touch with everything and everybody.

When Virginia reached old age, she became concerned about the meaning and measure of her life, and she again tried to connect with her neighbors in Hawkinsville and to the people and places of her youth in Mt. Zion. She began to attend the church of her childhood in Mt. Zion and to take part in the church's social functions and activities of benevolence. Occasionally she would be seen at civic events in both communities. Mrs. Virginia Garr was doing all that she could to re-connect, but unfortunately most everything had passed her by.

ooooo ◆ ooooo

When gifted Faye Sears entered high school, things slowed down somewhat for him, but he continued with his good grades and academic success. The big change for Faye was his new found reluctance to adhere to the rules: he began to show up late, he refused certain assignments, and he developed an inclination to question the school rules. These minor discretions didn't seem to cause the young man much trouble, and his sterling reputation and quick wit got him through high school without any major problems.

After his graduation, Faye Sears enrolled into the State University. He was one of a very few adolescents of Hamilton County able to attend the University, but college life didn't go well for the young man. He was suspended and then kicked out after only one year. He ran wild from the first day. It was at the college that he was introduced to beer, lost his innocence, and gave up all commitment to responsibility.

Early in the summer following Faye's year in college, he promptly got Yvonne Wells pregnant. Yvonne came from a poor and broken family of notorious slackers, and although she too was somewhat irresponsible, she was not nearly as unstable as Lafayette Sears. Yvonne and Faye were hurriedly married, took up drinking heavily at night, and mostly fought, slept, drank, and fought some more. The couple stayed together until their child, Annie, was about a year old. It was then, and nobody around Mt. Zion really knew why, that Yvonne deserted Sears and the girl. She left the farm country, moved to somewhere near Cincinnati, and was rarely ever heard from after that.

From that moment on, Lafayette Sears' life was punctuated by a series of unproductive and questionable changes. He lost the bank teller job that was given to him through his family connections. To make ends meet, which he was never really able to do, he began helping out on the farms around the county. The bill collectors and the landlord were always at his door. Sears began a pattern of moving with his young but growing daughter from one ramshackle tenant house to another. He was constantly getting rid of one worn out wreck of a car or pickup and trading for another of the same condition. He began to drink more heavily and in a short time became hopelessly addicted.

If there was one thing that was consistent in Faye Sears's broken life, it was his propensity for taking up with one disreputable woman after another. As soon as one would pack up and leave, Faye wasted no time in looking for another to move in with him and take her place. He was often heard saying that the women in his life were "hot and spicy," but the ladies around Hamilton County were more apt to refer to them as "tramps."

Life never improved for "Faye" Sears. He drifted from job to job and house to house. When the farmers of Hamilton County needed a casual laborer, they would usually call on Faye Sears. He was a dependable hand in the hay and tobacco fields, and he could be counted on as long as he started the day sober. If Faye was on a drunk, and that was certainly not a rare thing, he was basically incapacitated.

The bad days outnumbered the good ones, and eventually he became so undependable that people quit calling on him to help. He began to live off borrowed money, charity, and handouts from his family. In a move of complete irresponsibility, Lafayette Sears left his eleven year old daughter and followed some floozy to Ohio. He was jailed on charges of child abandonment, and eventually sent to prison.

Life after prison was no better for "Faye" than life before had been. He just took up where he left off. His reputation, his values, and his health were systematically destroyed. Finally, Lafayette Sears died in his sleep at the age of thirty nine.

ooooo◆ooooo

On the other hand, when the young brother, Lawrence Sears, was passed to grade five in the little elementary school, his life took a turn for the better. He was no longer exposed to Virginia Ashberry's humiliation, and he began to move in a direction far different from the destructive patterns of his brother. School life became a great deal more pleasant for the boy, and he began to come out of his shell. He was getting some positive attention and encouragement. For the first time in Lawrence's school career the young man began to apply himself to his studies. This change was certainly helped by his fifth grade teacher; Ms. Julia Browning.

Julia Browning was a young and enthusiastic second year teacher when Lawrence Sears entered her class. She immediately recognized that the boy was immature, withdrawn, and a little backwards. She encouraged Lawrence from the onset and never missed a chance to demonstrate to the young student that she had serious confidence in his abilities. It became apparent that there was nothing lacking with Lawrence's intelligence, and by the end of the school year, the young student was doing better than average with his schoolwork.

As Lawrence progressed through grades six, seven, and eight, his academic accomplishments improved with each passing grade. By the time he was ready to graduate from the elementary school and move on to the high school in Hawkinsville, Lawrence Sears was near the top half of his class. He not only was completing assignments and doing them well, but he was taking a genuine interest in his studies as well.

Lawrence's studies were not the only thing going through a notable change. After Ms. Browning's magical work, it seemed that with the passing of each day Lawrence's self esteem improved. He was becoming much less withdrawn, and he began to engage with his classmates in a friendly and somewhat teasing way. By the time Lawrence headed to the high school, he was one of the more popular students in his class.

High school life for Lawrence Sears was a little bitter and a little sweet. The first two years were somewhat of a struggle. The young man was paying a big price for the negligence of Ms. Virginia Ashberry and the misperceptions of some of his other early teachers. He had to apply himself and work extra hard to overcome some deficiencies in the foundations of his earliest academic development. Some of his classmates from Rock Creek and most of the students from the larger elementary school in Hawkinsville were better prepared to handle the more arduous class work that they were experiencing at the high school.

Lawrence faced the challenge with an unyielding perseverance: he was determined in his pursuit of stellar academic accomplishment. Each day the young man not only completed all of his homework assignments but continued to read and study until late at night. By the beginning of his junior year, Lawrence was at the top. The schoolwork became easier for him, and his life became more relaxing. When comments or insinuations were made that suggested that Lawrence was not only a top student but super-smart as well, the young man suppressed the smile that would have revealed his sense of pride.

It wasn't only at school that Lawrence developed a new sense of responsibility. At home he adhered to the everyday rules that were set down for him, and he was conscientious in the performance of his chores. His parents didn't have to worry too much about where he was or what he was doing. As Faye Sears slipped further into the abyss of his problems, Lawrence became an increasingly larger source of pride for his parents.

During Lawrence's sophomore year in high school the young man took the job of delivering the Lexington newspaper each morning. The papers were dropped off early in front of the post office in Hawkinsville. Lawrence would wake early, ride his bike the four miles from his home in Mt. Zion to Hawkinsville, pick up the newspapers, and make the home deliveries. When he finished the deliveries in Hawkinsville, he went back to Mt. Zion and delivered papers to a few customers there.

One irony that came with the paper route was that Virginia Ashberry Garr lived in Hawkinsville and took the morning paper. The two rarely met because the old teacher mailed the payment to the newspaper office. When their paths did cross, Virginia treated Lawrence with disregard and indifference. It was obvious that she still didn't care for the young man. Often Lawrence found himself wishing that his old teacher would ask him how he was doing so that he could brag about his good grades, his performance on the school debate team, or his having been elected a class officer. But Virginia was so sure of Lawrence's uselessness that she wasn't about to waste her breath asking the young man about anything. She didn't care for Lawrence, and it would be safe to assume that the young man wasn't exactly in love with her.

When Lawrence Sears graduated from Hawkinsville High School, things for the young man were as good as they get. He had graduated near the top of his class and received accolades and awards. Lawrence was popular with his peers, and his politeness endeared him to the adults of the community. He was an intelligent, mature, and sensitive young man.

The summer after graduation was a good one for Lawrence Sears. He had already been accepted at the State University, and he had until fall to prepare to leave for Lexington. Lawrence kept his paper route and worked around Mt. Zion helping neighbors and relatives in the hayfields and tobacco patches. Graduation had eliminated the pressure of studies in the evenings, and after supper each night Lawrence and the other young men and women of the area indulged in the carefree practice of just "hanging out." It was a carefree time.

The college experience for Lawrence was in no way like that of his older brother. Lawrence entered the College of Arts and Science with a major in pre-law. From the onset, he excelled in the academics. He joined a fraternity, dated the most attractive and popular girls, and was elected as an officer of the University Student Government.

Lawrence Sears graduated from the university in four years. He had already been accepted into the university law school and planned to just work around, relax and unwind at home in Mt. Zion during the summer break. It was a gratifying time for Lawrence Sears. During the day, he worked in the fields helping Jake Barnes and John Lewis, and at night, he hung out with Peachy Cornett and other old high school friends. On his visits to Hawkinsville that summer, Lawrence Sears always looked around to see if he could spot Virginia Ashberry Garr, but their paths never crossed. The young man had a driving wish to tell her of his success. Lawrence knew that his prideful compulsion to confront the old teacher with his accomplishments certainly bordered on being mean spirited, but he just couldn't help himself. Lawrence wanted her to know how wrong she had been about him. The old teacher had cruelly misjudged the young man, and some degree of resentment would remain with him for life.

Lawrence's relaxing summer ended with the coming of autumn. From the first day at law school it was obvious that the young man wasn't going to slow down one bit on his drive to the top. His grades were tops in his class, and he had the respect of the professors and the students alike. Lawrence graduated with honors in the prescribed three years and aced the bar exam the following summer.

The graduate didn't have to wait long to find employment. He was immediately hired by the prestigious Lexington law firm of McRay and Cole. Lawrence Sears wasted no time in proving his intelligence and his abilities, and in a short few years he was made a partner of the law firm. Lawrence's accomplishments had been astonishing.

He had reached the top professionally at a young age and was considered by all to be a kind and generous man.

ooooo ◆ ooooo

The death of LaFayette Sears came as no shock to the folks of Hamilton County. He had abused his body for his entire adult life. The causes of his downfall and his demise had become a topic of conversation and speculation over the years, and although it seemed inevitable that his life would end in tragedy, the community was not prepared for his early death. Karl and Anna Sears were the recipients of a great outpouring of sympathy and condolences.

On the night of Faye Sears's visitation, Grady's Funeral Home was a crowded place. Lawrence Sears had not left his parents' side except to casually visit with old friends who showed up to visit with him. He was talking with Peachy Cornett when he first spotted his old teacher, Mrs. Virginia Ashberry Garr. Lawrence was overcome with a mixture of emotions: part of him didn't want to even speak to his old teacher, but another equal element was driving him to confront the old lady. Mrs. Ashberry Garr eliminated his options when she noticed Lawrence and began to make her way in his direction.

"Well Lawrence," she said when she approached Lawrence, "I'm so sorry about your brother."

"Thank you ma'am. And thank you for coming."

"It's such a sad thing. And him so young," she said.

"Yes it is," said Lawrence. He thought that she was the oldest looking person he had ever seen.

It was at this moment that she did it: the old teacher asked Lawrence what he was doing with himself.

Lawrence hesitated for a moment and then thought to himself: *Well here goes. You've waited a long time for this, so you might as well just let it go.*

Lawrence briefly told his old teacher that he had attended the State University, graduated from law school, and was an attorney in Lexington. He could feel some anger rising, and he was somewhat surprised by that.

Ms. Ashberry Garr then said, "I always knew you were going to achieve special things."

"Well I…." Lawrence tried to speak.

"From your earliest days, you always had so much

talent," she added after interrupting Lawrence.

You've got to be kidding, he thought.

"But your brother always worried me." She said. "He just struggled so in the classroom."

Lawrence was speechless.

"He was my paperboy you know"

There was a long silence before Lawrence said, "Thanks for coming Mrs. Ashberry."

Firewood

"Didn't you try to stop him?" Jake Barnes asked.

"We did, we all did, Jake. We told him we'd help him with it, but he insisted and left."

The scene unfolded at the card table in McBride's Store. Several men were playing euchre, and Jake Barnes had just entered the store. McBride's was the nerve center of the tiny community of Mt. Zion, Kentucky; it was here that news was passed, gossip was shared, and things were left by one to be picked up by another. Jake was expressing his confusion as to why his brother-in-law, Farley Lamb, had loaded his riding mower unto a trailer, gassed up at the store, and was driving all the way to Lexington to have its oil changed.

ooooo ◆ ooooo

Farley Lamb had lived his entire life in the city. He met Jake Barnes's sister, Sarah, when they were both attending City College. They were married shortly after their graduation but continued to live in the city while Farley attended dental school. Both husband and wife had been looking forward to moving to a permanent home somewhere near her family and her childhood home. When a small dental practice came up for sale in Hawkinsville, they jumped at the chance, borrowed the money, bought the business, and began to look for a house. The search didn't last long; they found a nice small home in Mt. Zion, went to the bank again, bought the house, and settled in. The short four mile drive from Mt. Zion to Hawkinsville was no problem. Theirs was to be a life of country bliss.

Although Lamb was a polite and pleasant man and was accepted outwardly by most everyone, he didn't exactly fit in with all of the locals of Hamilton County. He seemed a little stuffy. Some would say that Farley thought he was a little better than everyone else, but of course that was just conjecture. Jake Barnes and his family believed that a certain degree of jealousy was behind the negative thoughts, and that he was just a little different. There were times, however, when Jake couldn't help himself and would tease, and tease some more, about Farley's signature ineptness.

Farley Lamb did not apply himself to the everyday work around the house and farm as did the majority of the men who resided in the county. Until old age slowed them down, the men of Mt. Zion took pride in doing their own repairs and maintenance. Neighbors were called to help with any two-man job. The men repaired the broken window pane, painted the screen door, put a roof on the garage, and ran the wire for a new outlet. Their wives canned, sewed, tended the garden, and they too would paint the screen door. There was a certain sense of pride and independence in being able to take care of oneself in this manner, but somehow Farley Lamb was not touched by that spirit. Doing for oneself was an important measure of character for the populace, and those who either couldn't or chose not to were looked upon with a subtle disdain.

If it was broke, Farley paid someone to repair it, and he surely never had a paintbrush in his hand. It was said teasingly that he didn't know the difference between a screwdriver and a hammer. There was no way Farley Lamb would know how to change the oil in his lawn mower, and there was little chance he was about to learn. For him, it was just much easier to take the mower to the dealer and have them service it. Farley was completely comfortable with his methods and seemed totally unaware that anyone might believe that somehow he didn't quite measure up.

ooooo ◆ ooooo

Jake Barnes lived with his wife and two sons in the tiny hamlet of Mt. Zion Kentucky. His daytime job was at the post office in Hawkinsville, but his time during the late afternoons and on weekends was devoted to the labors of tending to his hill farm. Hardly a day passed that Jake didn't drive the five miles from his home to his old farm. It was there with the help of his sons, Henry and Al, that he raised a tobacco crop and ran a few head of cattle to hack out a little extra spending money.

Jake was friendly by nature. There were two things that his friends and neighbors could be assured of when they encountered Jake: he would be smiling and would find something to tease about. Usually the teasing was directed towards the person he had just encountered. Jake was well liked and respected, and his teasing was not taken seriously. Jake had a way of making people smile.

To Jake, teasing was not the same as making fun of people, but sometimes the line of differentiation was not clear. If the subject of Jake's banter was not present, his joking could be viewed as ridicule. When his critical, but humorous, comments were directed towards a family member, no matter how distant, Jake's wife, Eloise, was quick to cut him off with the old "If you can't say anything nice, don't say anything at all" admonishment. It was then that Jake knew it was time for silence.

In spite of their differences, Jake Barnes had developed somewhat of a feeling of kindness blended with a sense of responsibility for his brother-in-law. From the beginning, the two were thrown together frequently: Jake had always been close to his younger sister, and that closeness didn't diminish with her marriage to Lamb. On his visits to Sarah's home, Jake might make a minor repair, fix a leaky faucet, or oil a squeaky door hinge. It wasn't uncommon for Farley himself to call Jake to help him with some project around the house, and Jake rather enjoyed the companionship that had developed. But one thing would never really change: Jake would always tease.

○○○○○◆○○○○○

The dental practice of Farley Lamb grew rapidly. He was a capable dentist, and his pleasant nature attracted clients to his office. With the growth of his business came a substantial increase in income, and with the money came a change in how the Lambs perceived their needs. Farley and his wife were able to relax a little about how they managed their money. Going out to eat was no longer a painful experience, and purchases that had been considered luxurious before became everyday events. After their first child was born, the couple decided that it was time to buy or build a larger house.

When the Morgan place on the edge of town came up for sale, the pair jumped at the chance to buy it. During the early part of the twentieth century, Abe Morgan had made a fortune in New Orleans shipping grains and feeds. In his old age, he retired, moved back to his childhood farm in Mt. Zion, and built a larger than practical two story brick home. After Morgan's death, the big house went through a long series of owners, and with each, it fell a little further into disrepair. For one solid year following their purchase, the Lambs hired contractors, painters, plumbers, and electricians to put the old mansion into top shape.

The Farley's moved into their new home in late fall of their fifth year of living in Mt. Zion. The housewarming dinner was extraordinary: most everyone who lived around Mt. Zion was present. The contractors who had worked on the old place were all there. Everyone was having a gay old time. When Lamb was giving a tour of his new home to some of the guests, Jake Barnes couldn't keep from wondering how his brother-in-law would ever keep up with the maintenance on such a large house. When Jake asked Farley about the upkeep, the new owners' reply was, "I'll just have to keep these contractors close from now on."

From the onset, it was out in the big yard around the house that Farley had dreams of becoming a farmer. The old mansion had a considerable yard that surrounded the home. It was the kind of place that people referred to as "grounds" rather than a yard. Farley Lamb had big ambitions: the old horse stable was rebuilt to store his new riding mower, weed eaters, garden tools, and every other gizmo and machine imaginable. Farley's goal was to keep the grounds manicured and to plant and grow a substantial garden. His wife, Sarah, encouraged him and suggested that she would freeze and can whatever Farley's garden produced.

In early spring, Farley Lamb was excited about mowing and weed-eating his big yard. A warm Saturday offered the perfect time to get started. He started right off on his new mower but hadn't gone far before he realized that limbs had broken and fallen from the trees during the winter months; he would have to pick them up and establish a burn pile before he could continue with the mowing. As the homeowner worked on the limbs, he noticed how much paper and debris had blown in, and he saw that it too would have to be picked up before he could mow.

It was late morning before Farley got back on his mower, and he was already about half exhausted. Farley Lamb finished mowing in the mid afternoon. He hadn't had lunch, his behind was sore from riding the mower, and he wasn't exactly real happy at that moment. After a quick sandwich, he tackled the job of weed-eating, which he was sure he could complete in about thirty minutes. After weed-eating, he could then be done for the day and go inside to watch the Cincinnati Red's on television. But once again he hit a major snag: the weeds around the trees, outbuildings, and parts of the house had been allowed to grow so big that they were too tough for the weed-eater to handle. Each time he tried, the string broke. Farley became increasingly more and more frustrated until finally he gave up, threw the weed-eater into the storage building, and went to the sofa. As soon as he got home from church the next afternoon, he called his neighbor Haywood Shedd to see if Haywood's son, Artie, could cut out the old weeds, and that was the end of Farley Lamb's weed-eating endeavors.

Despite the weed-eating experience, Farley Lamb maintained a certain enthusiasm for his huge yard. He was looking forward to putting out the garden, and when warm dry weather came with May, Farley could hardly wait to get out his new rotor-tiller and begin plowing up the huge and long abandoned garden space. It didn't take more than a few moments before Farley realized that rotor-tilling through the grass sod that had taken over the garden wasn't anything like the easy work as shown on the T.V. commercials. The tiller bounced, jerked, and was impossible to steer. After about five minutes, Farley Lamb's arms felt like they were going to fall off, his right knee was out of place, and his head was throbbing. With a sigh, he shut off the tiller and went inside to call his brother-in-law, Jake, to see if he could help.

Jake's little 8N Ford tractor was perfect for the job. When he finished plowing and harrowing up the garden space, he offered to help his brother-in-law set out the garden, but Farley insisted on doing it himself. What Jake knew but Farley Lamb didn't know was that putting in a garden required the use of muscles that weren't used much, and soreness was certain to follow. Farley went ahead with his plans to set out the garden himself. He spent the whole day on Saturday marking off the rows, planting the seeds for beans, peas, and corn, and setting out the pepper and tomato plants and the onion sets. The constant bending over and going from his knees to standing up was exhausting, and by the time Farley got to the job of planting the seed potatoes, he could hardly move.

Farley Lamb was able to get to work the next day, but that was about the extent of it. For three mornings, he could hardly get out of bed, and he limped around for over a week. Like a lot of newcomers to the garden business, Farley believed that when the seeds were planted, the job was done. All he had to do after planting was merely indulge in the plentiful harvest when the time was right. Of course his perception led to a total disaster: plants shriveled from lack of water, the bugs and critters feasted, and the weeds took over.

Before long, the folks passing by could no longer see Farley's garden. The weeds had grown so tall that they covered everything else. Around the neighborhood, Farley's garden disaster became the subject of some gossipy comments and a little mild teasing. Jake himself was sometimes teased about his brother in law, and when that happened, Jake mostly just grinned and made no comment. At the Barnes' dinner table one evening, Jake made a joking comment about Farley's idea that a few weeks after the seeds were in the ground, Farley expected to walk into his garden and pick up a few cans of stewed tomatoes. Before there was even the slightest snicker, Jake's wife snapped her head around and gave a stare to Jake and their two sons that would have stopped a truck: there was to be no teasing about Farley Lamb in her presence.

ooooo◆ooooo

The Barnes family Thanksgiving dinner that year had the usual family and guests. In addition to Jake and Eloise Barnes and their two sons, Henry and Al, there were the Lambs and Jake's cousins, Bee Jay and Harold Browning. There had been a sharp cold snap, but the day was bright and beautiful. Jake's home was old and spacious, and there was plenty of room for everyone. The men were sitting around in the large living room, and the women were in the kitchen making the final preparations for the meal. The Lamb's young daughter was all over the house.

On this particular Thanksgiving Day, Jake Barnes had a fire burning in the living room fireplace. A distinguishing feature of the fireplace was its small size. Old homes that were constructed in the 1890's had fireplaces built to burn lump coal and not the huge logs of earlier fireplaces. The coal grates that were fitted into the fireplaces could only accommodate a piece of firewood no longer than about ten inches.

Jake always had a supply of the undersized fire wood stacked neatly on his porch. He would cut the wood on his old farm sometime in October and take a pickup load to his home when the stack got low. Fallen trees and deadfalls where abundant, and finding wood to cut was never a problem. Jakes adult sons, Al and Henry, both burned wood as well. During October and early November, they made the trip from their homes in Lexington to Mt. Zion to work with Jake cutting, splitting, and stacking the wood. The work was difficult, exhausting, and backbreaking, but in spite of that, the men enjoyed their time together. It had become somewhat of a family tradition.

On this particular Thanksgiving afternoon, Jake, Al, Henry, Farley, and the Browning brothers were sitting in the living room engaged in mostly meaningless conversation. They were enjoying the warmth of the fire. Jake got up to toss another of the small logs into the fireplace, and it was at that exact moment that Farley Lamb asked one of the all time dumbest questions ever asked:

"Where did you ever find firewood that size, Jake?" asked Farley Lamb.

Jake stood perfectly still for a few seconds. Al and Henry both snapped their heads around and looked directly at Jake to see what kind of smart assed teasing retort their father would come back with. The room was silent. But Jake was touched by the sweet spirit of the holiday, and also, since his back was to the kitchen door and he wasn't exactly sure where his wife might be, he decided to just let it go.

"The boys and I cut it, Farley," was his simple reply.

ooooo ◆ ooooo

The next summer Al and Henry were up from Lexington to help their father with his hay baling. Peachy Cornett and Bee Jay Browning showed up as well. It was a brutally hot and humid August day with absolutely no breeze, and the men knew that they were in for a punishing time. Jake Barnes had square baled the hay the day before, and the work remaining was the tough job of loading the hay onto wagons and then ricking it up in the old tobacco barn. Loading the hay was the easier of the two challenges.

Jake drove the tractor slowly through the fields pulling a wagon behind. Two men stood on the wagon and stacked the bales. The other men walked beside the wagon and threw the square bales up onto the wagon and to the stackers. When the wagon was loaded as full as they could possibly get it, the men climbed on the wagons wherever they could and made the trip to the barn.

After a visit to the water spigot and a short break, the men headed to the barn where the real work began. Unlike the outside labor of loading the bales onto the wagons, there was no air moving around the men in the barn. It was hot, dirty, and dusty. The day was so humid that Henry complained that it was like breathing "liquid air." A man on the wagon handed the hay bale to the men on the ground, and they in turn carried it and tossed it up to the men stacking it high in the barn. After about one minute, they were all soaking wet from perspiration. The men began to cough from breathing the dust. It was the meanest work on the farm. Occasionally, one of the men would have to stop for a couple of minutes to rest and catch his breath. The others just shifted their tasks to accommodate the recuperating worker: there was no teasing.

The men were on their third or fourth load when it happened. By that time, they were totally drained, sore, and short tempered. They were almost finished unloading and stacking the load when Al shouted from high up in the barn, *"Hey Jake, where'd you ever get firewood that size?"*

Every man in the barn burst out laughing.

Case Closed

It was an early Sunday morning in October, and John Lewis was doing what he did almost every morning. He was driving the short distance from his big river bottom farm just north of Mt. Zion to check on the cattle he had on his sister's place two miles south of the hamlet. As he was passing through the little village, he spotted Haywood Shedd sitting on his front porch. He was surprised to see Haywood up so early, and he reasoned that since he hadn't seen the gentleman for some time, he would stop, visit for a few minutes, and maybe catch up on a little news.

Lewis pulled over to the side of the road, got out of his pickup, and walked the few steps up to Shedd's porch. "What's up buddy? You're up kinda early aren't you? Didn't you go with them last night?"

"That's three questions, John," Haywood Shedd answered. "So I'll just answer them in the order that you fired them off to me. Not much, couldn't sleep, and yes I was there. Want a cup of coffee?"

"No thanks," John answered, and then asked, "Well, how'd Jake do? How'd Ole Blue do? How'd it come out?"

ooooo ◆ ooooo

Ole Blue was Jake Barnes's prized coon hound. The old dog was considered to be the best to come along in many years, and that bit of regard gave both Jake and Ole Blue some extra standing around the county. The year was 1976, and the hunting of raccoons was still very much in vogue with a certain group of men. "Coon huntin'" was big sport in Hamilton County, and hardly a night passed that somebody wasn't out with the hounds.

There was a spirit of competition involved on their jaunts into, and through, the woods. The men were given to bragging about the skills of their favorite hounds during the day, but when night came, it was the time of reckoning. An atmosphere of good natured rivalry followed. The nights commenced with each man trying to prove the worth of his most trusted hound. Each man's mind was set on proving that his daytime bragging about the abilities of his old Redbone or the potential of his young Bluetick was warranted and not just a lot of useless chatter.

But when an outsider showed up from another county to challenge the areas top hounds, the competitive spirits cranked up. Almost always the local hunters would know of the top hounds from around the area, even those three and four counties away. It was in no way unusual for these challenges to take place, and sometimes they were planned weeks in advance. The men had plenty of time and plenty of words to play and replay how the night would go.

ooooo ◆ ooooo

To be successful, the coon hunter and the coon hound both had to have some exceptional and rare abilities. Each had talents that were normally not understood and mostly unappreciated by the non-hunting public. They were a select group whose fascination with their sport had its foundation in generations of conditioning.

All of the hounds, whether they were the Blue Tick, Redbone, Walker, or Black and Tan, had an extraordinary sense of smell. The hounds could smell the track of any animal that had passed, even if it had been up to two hours earlier. The good hounds were trained to only bark when they smelled the trail of a raccoon. They had better not even whimper if they came upon the trail of a possum, skunk, house-cat or deer. To top it off, they were so skilled that they could determine in a few seconds which direction the varmint had traveled. It was then that they began to bark and bawl intermittently as they worked together in their effort to catch the raccoon. The drive of the hounds was astonishing. When the raccoon got tired or the hounds got too close, the coon would climb the biggest tree and peer down at the barking hounds. The hound dogs all changed their bark when they were "treed". The bark became more of a chop and less of a bawl. The distinction was easy to determine even by the least experienced hunter. The last job of the good hound was to stay on the tree until the hunter arrived, even if it took hours or days.

The hunter himself had to have special talents too. Training the hounds took intelligence and patience. The men were able to identify the dogs by their barks usually after hearing them only once. The hunters knew which dogs were leading in the hunt. Mostly, the men of the woods knew exactly what the coon was doing to elude the hounds and precisely what the dogs were doing in response. They were so good at it that there was rarely any sort of disagreement over which dogs were doing what.

Perhaps the most distinctive skill of the coon hunter himself was his ability to stay out in the woods all night in all sorts of bad weather and not complain or come down with illness. To top it off, the hunter would get up and go to work the next morning after spending half the night in the woods. But surely, the most amazing skill of the night hunter was his ability to stay out night after night, come in muddy and tired, and still somehow remain blissfully married year after year.

ooooo ◆ ooooo

Jake Barnes was in his early forties when he inherited Ole Blue. A distant cousin had died up in West Union, Ohio, and his widow begged Jake to take the old dog. She was going to sell their home and move to Florida, and all she wanted with the dog was to be rid of it.

Jake was not a coon hunter. He had been with the men a couple of times when he was a boy but never took up the sport. He worked at the post office in Hawkinsville and farmed on the side. His time was consumed with work. He was not one bit excited about taking the dog, but in a mood of sympathy and benevolence, he loaded the old hound up and headed back to Kentucky.

Barnes did not live on his farm but made the four mile trip daily to feed his cattle, work the crop, or just check on things. He added to his daily list of tasks the feeding and watering of Ole Blue. The farmer had fixed up a dog house and put it inside his tobacco barn, and the hound was kept on a light lead chain that was fastened to a tier rail right above the dog's house. The old hound would just lie there and hardly even look up when Jake tended to him.

It was early and bright one October Saturday morning when Jake Barnes changed things up a little. The old hound had let out a slight whine and wagged his tale when the farmer finished pouring his feed and had turned to walk away. Without really giving it much thought, Jake reached down and unhooked the dog from his chain. The old hound stood still for about ten seconds and then bounded through the barn door and ran out the ridge sniffing and zig-zagging until he disappeared over the rise near the end of the ridge. Jake Barnes just shrugged: the dog would surely return.

As was always the case, Jake had his work lined out for the day. Usually he used his old Massey Ferguson tractor and an ancient two wheeled work trailer to carry out the countless small maintenance and repair jobs that were always there, and this day would be no exception. When Jake had his tools loaded, he took the tractor and trailer and headed out to check fence and cut a little firewood. He went in the opposite direction to that of the dog.

It was quiet, and Jake Barnes was enjoying the solitude. As he had suspected, a recent storm had snapped two big limbs that had smashed a line fence. It would be an easy job to cut and remove the limbs, pull the fence up, and drive a steel post in to reinforce the weakened fence. Jake Barnes had hardly begun when he was startled by the presence of Ole Blue. The old dog just walked up, sat down, and hung around Jake while he worked for the rest of the morning.

In a short time, Jake Barnes and his old hound became almost inseparable. The dog would be by his side when Jake was at his farm, and soon the tier rail chain was abandoned. Ole Blue was free to roam but was always there to greet Barnes when he drove into the farm drive. Before too long, Ole Blue was traveling in the back of Jake's pickup, and it got to where if you saw one you surely would see the other.

ooooo ◆ ooooo

Almost every little crossroads community in Kentucky had a small mom and pop grocery or general store. It was a place to pick up a sack of victuals, a pound of nails, or a sandwich and chips for lunch. Often there was a group of the local men gathered around the wood stove talking or sitting around a table playing a game of euchre or Rook. "Loafers" was the universal word for describing these fellows, but that was generally an unfair expression.

They were mostly hard working men and sometimes women, who were just taking a break or catching up on some news. All the comings and goings of local interest were passed along from mouth to mouth at the store. The first question asked by most everybody who entered was something along the lines of, "What's the latest?" The stores served as the nerve centers of the small communities.

McBride's was a small grocery and farm supply store at the northeast crossroads corner in the little town of Mt. Zion, Kentucky. On this particular rainy Saturday afternoon, about half of the "loafer" population happened to be enthusiastic coon hunters.

The conversation moved to Jake Barnes and Ole Blue when Haywood Shedd said, "I still think I'd like to see what Jake's Blue Tick can do. Something about that dog makes me think he'll hunt."

"I've asked Jake to go two or three times, but he won't go," said Bee Jay Browning.

"Let's see if he'll let us take the dog with us tonight. Maybe he will."

"Bullshit! He isn't going to let that dog out of his sight," spoke up Eulous Hobbs.

"Well, let's go see anyway," said Shedd, "We're not

doing anything anyhow."

"Yeah, might as well. Let's go," said Bee Jay. And the men left the store for the short drive to Jake's place.

ooooo◆ooooo

The trio found Jake Barnes working on a sickle mower in his barn. The farmers around Mt. Zion usually saved a few straightening up and fixing jobs to be done inside the barn on rainy days. The rain gave the farmers a little change of pace and for the most part a more relaxing day. Feeding or checking on the livestock was followed by the inside jobs and then a trip to town to get whatever was needed to complete the work.

When Jake looked up and saw Haywood Shedd, Bee Jay Browning, and Eulous Hobbs coming into his barn, he burst out laughing. "This can't be good," he said. "What's going on, more coon dog stuff?"

"Yeah, we're all going tonight and want you to go with us," said Browning.

"Or if you can't go, let us hunt your old dog and see what he can do," added Hobbs.

"You guys are persistent. You're all crazy; can you not see the rain?" said Jake Barnes.

"Supposed to stop. We won't go if it doesn't," said Hobbs.

Jake signaled for Bee Jay to lift the mower bar up and get it level so he could pull the sickle out. While he was tugging on the sickle, he looked up and said, "All right. All right. I'll go."

"Good….Great. We'll pick you up at your place, Jake, and we'll have a good light for you," said Bee Jay Browning.

Jake smiled and said somewhat sarcastically, "I can hardly wait."

The three visitors laughed, piled into their pickup, and left. Jake went back to his work.

∞∞∞∞◆∞∞∞∞

The rain did stop, and the hunt was on. The three men pulled into Jake's drive with two pickup trucks, each with a dog box in the back. When Jake unhooked Ole Blue, the hound dashed to the nearest truck. Haywood Shedd let down the tailgate and opened the small door to the dog box. Without coaxing, Ole Blue jumped onto the tailgate and loaded like he had done it ten thousand times before.

It was a short drive to Norris's woods, and that is where the men decided to put out the dogs. There was very little undergrowth in the big woods, and the land lay mostly level. Walking was not difficult. Haywood Shedd figured that since they had talked Jake into going with them, they might as well make it as easy as possible on the novice night hunter.

When the men let the four hounds out, they bounded to a slight ravine and raced straight down into the woods. In two or three minutes, Ole Blue opened up with a long bawl. The men had never heard Jake's hound before, but they knew at once that it was Ole Blue because it was a new sound to them.

"That's you Jake. Wonder what he's got," said Bee Jay Browning.

There was a moment of silence while the men waited for one of the other hounds to join in the chase. Until a "straight cooner" barked and confirmed that Ole Blue was in fact tracking a raccoon, there was room for skepticism. Then Eulous Hobbs's Redbone, Drupe, came in with his unmistakable gravelly bawl, and within a few seconds more all four hounds were barking and bawling wide open.

"You're out in front Jake," said Bee Jay. "He's definitely not slow."

When Jake's hound "treed" first with a short loud

chopping bark all of the men were impressed. One after another, the other dogs joined in the serenade. The loud barking filled the night air and echoed off the adjacent hillsides. It was a beautiful sound to the hunters: a sound the old-time hunters called "mountain music." The men stood and listened for a few moments and then walked into the woods to get their dogs.

When they got to the huge white oak where the hounds were treed, they shined their lights into the top limbs of the big tree to try and spot the raccoon. "There he is," said Haywood when his bright Wheat Light found the raccoon. The critter's eyes reflected the light back down to the hunters like two beacons.

"Dang, Jake, that old hound's all right," said Hobbs as the men were making over their dogs for doing a good job.

The men began to hook their lead chains to the dogs' collars and led them away from the tree when Haywood Shedd added, "Looks to me like he's better than just 'all right.'"

The four hunters decided to go a little further into the woods and see if they could hit the track of another raccoon. They led the hounds away from the tree, let them loose, and sent them down into a dry creek bed. It took a little longer this time, but the scenario played out almost exactly as it had the first time. Jake's old hound had the first "strike" and was the first to tree. Once again, the hunters were able to see the critter and confirm that it was in fact a raccoon. They were all impressed: almost in disbelief.

The four men called it an evening, loaded the hounds into their trucks, and headed to their homes. It was then that the talk began. They were astonished at Ole Blue's performance.

"It looks like you might really have something there," said Eulous Hobbs.

"Unbelievable," said Haywood Shedd.

"Jake, where in the Hell did he come from?" asked Bee Jay Browning.

And on and on went the accolades and conversation. Mostly Jake Barnes just listened, but he was digesting the realization that the evening had in no way been unpleasant. He was smiling on the inside and soaking it all up.

ooooo ◆ ooooo

Jake Barnes was hooked. It was only a few days before he was out in the woods again. The first night of hunting with Ole Blue had created within Jake

Barnes a thirst to go again. Like any endeavor, a little success breeds certain excitement, and with time the excitement grows. Haywood Shedd ran into Jake at the laundry in Hawkinsville and asked if he was ready to go again. Jake didn't hesitate: he had been eager and ready.

The three men followed the same procedure as they did in their first hunt together, but this time they took just one pickup. All three men piled into the front seat. Only a few seconds passed before Haywood said, "I brought my Redbone, Annie, with me tonight. We want to see how Ole Blue will stack up with her." And that began the long practiced tradition of night hunters challenging a good dog with increasingly more experienced and proven hounds.

The men decided to put out on Chandler Holmes's farm. It was an easy drive across the narrow ridges that made up Holmes's land, and the men could release the dogs right above Zeigler's Branch. They would have a high and dry place to listen for the hounds when they worked down the hillsides and into the small creek. They stopped at Chandler Holmes's house to ask permission, and they found Holmes and his wife listening to the radio. She was sewing and he was half asleep. Holmes was glad to see the men, and they shared a few minutes of small talk. Holmes wished the hunters luck, but refused the trio's invitation to join them.

The second night of hunting ended exactly as the first. Jake's hound easily out performed the other two hounds. The hunters treed two coons that night. On the first coon Haywood's hound found the cold track and opened up first. The trail was old, and the hounds had trouble working it out, but Ole Blue led most of the way and treed first. The second coon treed by the hounds was all Ole Blue from beginning to end. The two experienced night hunters were astonished, and Jake Barnes was once again smiling to himself.

The pattern was set and reversing it just wasn't going to happen. Old Blue was getting a reputation that spread quickly throughout the countryside. Hunters from around the county were anxious to try their hounds against the reputed skills of Ole Blue. Jake Barnes began to hunt on a regular basis, and never, not once, did the old hound fail.

ooooo ◆ ooooo

A.J. McAlister was a big time coon hunter from up in Vance County. He would keep anywhere from ten to twenty hounds in his kennels at one time.

McAlister was always buying, selling, and trading his dogs: that was about all he ever did. His latest addition, a Black and Tan named Jasper, was his pride and joy. He made it clear to anyone who would listen that, not only was Jasper the best hound he had ever owned, he was also surely the best that had ever lived.

It was only a matter of time before McAlister began to hear about the dog named Ole Blue from down in Hamilton County. The word was spreading that Old Blue was unbeatable in the woods: he was the hound dog equivalent of Superman. A.J. McAlister's ego and super self regard were threatened each time he heard of Ole Blue. His superiority in the hound dog business was being obliquely challenged, and that just wouldn't do. McAlister made his way down to tiny Mt. Zion one Saturday afternoon to find this man named Jake Barnes and his Blue Tick hound.

When McAlister entered McBride's store, he was boisterous and loud. Politeness was not a huge part of his makeup. "Do you know where I can find a Jake Barnes?" he asked the four men playing cards at the big table by the front window.

"And sir, who might you be?" asked Harold Browning.

"I'm A. J. McAlister from over in Vance County,"

the man said after puffing himself all up, "and I hear he's got a pretty good coon hound."

"Yeah, good. Real good," said Ernie Stone, "but I doubt if Jake'd ever sell the old hound."

"Sell? Hell! I don't want to buy him. I want to see if he's as good as they been say'n. I was hoping this Barnes guy would hunt with me and one of my good hounds, and we could see just how good his'n is."

"Come on, I'll drive you over to Jake's. I'm sure he'll be glad to see you," said Ernie Stone.

ooooo◆ooooo

Haywood Shedd and Eulous Hobbs went with the men that night of the big showdown. The men decided that Juett's Ridge was as good a place as any to begin the hunt. The hilltop ridge was flat and productive farm land. It was unusually large for that part of the country and covered about forty acres. The land was level on top, sloped off slightly on each side and then gave way to steep wooded hillsides that dropped to the two creeks that defined its boundaries. Sandy Fork Creek ran along the west side of the ridge and Elsie's Branch was on the east. The ridge was wide at its beginning by the highway and narrowed towards its northern end. It ended in a point where the two creeks merged into one.

A unique feature of Juett's Ridge was the ancient rock fence that split the big field into two segments. Towards the center of the big ridge and at its widest point, a wall began at the foot of the hill by one creek and ran continuously up the hillside across the open ridge and down the hill to the creek at the other side. There was a twenty foot break in the old fence right in the center of the field. The opening provided the access from one part of the field to the next. An old dirt and rock tobacco road passed through the break.

The men drove through the break in the rock wall and then a little further out the ridge. They parked and let the hounds out. Hobbs brought his Red Bone to hunt along with Ole Blue and McAlister's champion Black and Tan, Jasper. In about one minute the hounds hit a red hot track. The men must have turned the dogs out right on top of the coon. All three dogs were barking and bawling without catching their breath as they chased the coon down the hill on the men's left and then on to Sandy Fork Creek. The raccoon followed the creek down to the point where it met Elsie's Branch, and as he went in and out of the water, he was able to slow down the pursuit of the hounds. At first it was difficult for the hunters to determine which hound was leading the chase, but when they got into the water and had to work out the track, it became clear that McAlister's hound was a little quicker at it.

At the point where the two creeks met, the old coon turned and headed up Elsie's Branch. He kept in the water as much as he could and because of that was able to stay just ahead of the hounds. He was passing by the men down on their right when McAlister said, "Jasper's working through that water better than either one of you. He's doing the hard work." Jake, nor Eulous, nor Haywood commented.

The raccoon stayed just ahead of the hounds as it ran up through Elsie's Branch to the point behind the men where the stone wall began. It was there that the coon made an unusual move: he jumped up unto the wall and ran on its top and up the hill to where the wall broke for the old road. Walking on the wall was no trouble whatsoever for the coon but was impossible for the dogs: they had to stay on the ground and try to sort out the trail from there. The ploy of the coon slowed the dogs down so much that he was able to get a lot of distance between himself and the hounds.

"That's a smart old coon. He got on that old fence," said Haywood Shedd.

"Yeah, he ain't worried. He's just messing with them," said McAllister.

"But he'll get tired. He'll have to tree somewhere. He isn't going to lose these hounds," said Jake.

When the coon got to the break in the rock wall, he jumped down, ran the twenty feet to where the wall started again, and jumped right back up. He then traveled on the top of that part of the stone fence right back down to Sandy Fork where the whole chase had started. Again the coon headed down the creek towards Elsie's Branch. When the hounds finally worked out the rock wall problem and reached the bottom themselves, they were able to make up lost time. The dogs were again bawling and howling with every breath.

The coon got to the junction of the two creeks and again headed right back up Elsie's Branch to the rock wall. By then the hounds were right on his tail, but again the coon took the wall up the hill. The old coon was able to use the rock fence to distance himself from the dogs one more time. At the top, he jumped off for the twenty foot break, leaped back up, and once again took the wall right back down to Sandy Fork.

The three hounds were so close to each other that it was impossible to tell which was in the lead, but

Ole Blue and Hobbs's Redbone were both barking less and less: they were much older that McAlister's hound, and stamina was becoming a factor. Of course McAlister didn't miss a chance to point that out, "Your old dogs are almost spent, getting real tired."

When the coon came to Elsie's Branch and turned up the little creek for the third time, Ole Blue quit the track altogether: he became silent. A. J. McAlister laughed, Haywood Shedd grimaced, Eulous Hobbs shrugged, and Jake Barnes stood motionless. McAlister's hound and Hobbs' Red Bone continued the chase up Elsie's Branch. In less than a minute, the men all heard the jangle of Ole Blue's dog tags. The hunters shined their lights in the direction of the sound and immediately caught the bright reflection of Ole Blue's eyes. He was running up the ridge from where the two creeks joined and straight towards the men. When Ole Blue got to where the men were standing, he never even slowed down. He ran right by them and past the parked trucks. He continued straight on in the direction of the rock wall.

All three men had a faint suspicion of what Ole Blue was doing, but the notion was just too unbelievable. The hunters were thinking that maybe the old hound was going to the point of the twenty foot break in the wall to wait for that old coon. If the coon did in fact traverse the wall for a third time, it would be a terrible mistake. When he jumped off the wall at the break, he'd land right on top of Ole Blue, and that would be it for the chase and the coon. Not one of the three hunters said a word. McAlister began to shuffle his feet, Eulous Hobbs dropped his head and looked like he was praying, and Jake Barnes crossed his arms across his chest and stared in the direction of the rock wall.

When Hobbs' Redbone and McAlister's hound got to the wall where it met Elsie's Branch, the hunters knew instantly that the coon had taken the wall for a third time. Jake broke the silence when he said, "Well, we'll know in a minute."

"I don't believe this," said McAlister.

Eulous Hobbs whispered to himself, "Com'on Blue, Com'on Blue."

Then it happened. Coming from the direction of the rock wall was the most awful combination of growling, hissing, squalling, barking, and yelping ever heard. The noisy commotion stopped for about ten seconds before Ole Blue settled into an arithmetic treeing bark: chop, chop, chop. He was treeing with every breath.

The hunters got to Ole Blue about the same time as the other two hounds. They saw immediately what had happened: the old coon had gotten momentarily free from Ole Blue and dashed to the first thing he could find to climb up. He was at the top of a very small scrub oak tree and barely out of the reach of the barking hounds.

"Well, what about that?" Haywood Shedd said as the men led their hounds away from the raccoon.

"I can't believe… I've never…," stammered A. J. McAlister.

"Yeah, pretty good for a too old and too tired old hound, huh?" said Hobbs.

There was a moment's silence before McAlister said, "Yeah, gawd dangdest best hound dog move I ever saw."

"Yep," said Shedd, "the best. Period. Case closed!"

The Addition

There were two churches in Mt. Zion, Kentucky, and they had both been a part of the community since shortly after white man first set foot in the area. There was the Mt. Zion First Christian Church that sat on the pinnacle in the center of the little hamlet, and further down the highway, on the edge of town, there was the Mt. Zion Baptist Church. Mostly the citizenry could be divided into three groups and were to some degree identified in accordance to which assembly they did, or did not, belong. There was the Baptist group, the Christian group, and the didn't-go-at-all group.

When it was time for the annual softball game and the county fair cooking and canning competition, the Baptist and the Christian congregations carried on a spirit of good natured competition, but on all other occasions they were mostly gracious one to the other. When a fire destroyed part of the sanctuary at the Baptist Church, they were invited to use the Christian Church building for their services while the damaged building was being rebuilt. It was this kind of gesture that kept the community cemented to itself, and the Baptists were certainly appreciative.

The Baptist congregation chose not only to rebuild the damaged section, but they decided to erect a brand new and spacious addition as well. For the Christian Church flock, that's when the trouble began.

When it was completed, the new addition was nice and spacious, and the Baptist congregation was able to offer some services that would have been impossible before. Youth activities were easily accommodated, and more Sunday school classes were added without causing some cramping. Soon, the room was being used for receptions and banquets by organizations and clubs from outside the church. Of course, the natural result of this was a slight growth in the size of the Baptist congregation, and that was just fine with everyone except for one slight side effect: the Christian Church people were experiencing a corresponding reduction in their attendance.

At first the Christian Church members were only slightly concerned, but as their attendance numbers continued on a downward spiral, anxious conversations and worried contemplation gave way to a burst of panicky alarm. The solution was obvious: they'd just build a bigger addition than that of the Baptists. The proposition was promptly brought before the Church Board of Trustees, and all Hell broke loose.

ooooo◆ooooo

Most of the tobacco barns around Hawkinsville and Mt. Zion still had the leaf hanging from their rails. The job of stripping the cured tobacco leaves from the stalks had begun. Every farm had at least one barn with an attached "stripping" room where the monotonous and time consuming process took place. It was here that the local news was passed along during the slow work. The farmer, his neighbors, children, and possibly his wife would stand at the

benches and pass the days pulling the leaf and baling it according to color and condition. The leaves were put into presses and baled as the final step in the all-consuming labor of getting a crop from seeds to the market, and although it was slow work, there was always a little feeling of relief and a pleasant sense of finality. A wood stove and a crock-pot with soup or chili were standard features. A radio provided the background to the ongoing conversations, and no topic was off limits. The weather, crops, illnesses, and the high-school ball teams were always hot topics.

"How'd the meeting go?" Ernie Stone asked John Lewis as soon as John entered the stripping room. Both men had been helping Shorty Cornett get his crop stripped out.

John just shook his head and raised his shoulders in the familiar "who knows" gesture. The first meeting of the Christian Church Board of Trustees to discuss the building of the new addition had taken place the night before, and John Lewis was a trustee. There were very few secrets around Mt. Zion, and most everyone believed that the church leadership would simply and quickly vote to add on to their church. They had the room to grow, and they had the ability to raise the money.

There was about two minutes of silence before John

Lewis said, "Melvin Beasley is a hard no. He's against it, and it looks like he's going to be stubborn to the end. Melvin's going to be unyielding, hardheaded. Everybody else is either all for it or open to the idea. That hard head's going to be a problem. We couldn't really even talk. You know how Beasley can be."

ooooo ◆ ooooo

Melvin Beasley was the patriarch of a rather large outfit. In addition to his children and grandchildren, there were four or five additional families of cousins, nieces and nephews. The earliest Beasleys settled around the headwaters of Sandy Fork creek, and that's where they stayed. At one time there had been a small settlement named Beasley Town, but all signs of the little place were long gone. Even the old road that ran south from Hawkinsville, crossed the creek and connected with the Mt. Zion road was just a memory. The Beasleys tended a collection of marginal and hilly farms that lay at the end of a long gravel lane. The lane dropped off Thurman's Ridge and followed the bank of the creek until it ended at the last Beasley home.

Beasley and his outfit were known to be hard working and honest people. They were also considered to be backwards and somewhat peculiar. They stayed mostly to themselves and didn't really socialize when they did make it into town. The Beasley's identifying trademark was rapid speech and a high pitched nasal voice, and from time to time there was some teasing about that. However, in spite of their aloofness and odd behavior, the Beasleys were considered good people and were mostly well regarded. If their help was needed, they would show up in mass. As a rule though, except for church functions, they weren't seen much.

The Beasleys farmed hard and prayed hard. The family was known for their commitment to attendance at the Christian church and strict adherence to the fundamental principals of Christianity: every word of the bible was to be interpreted literally. Each Sunday they left their farmsteads, sometimes in a caravan, and headed to church as a group. They would wait around the parking lot until the entire family was there and then would enter the church and sit together. After church, they mixed with the rest of the congregation for a few minutes, exchanged pleasantries, and shared a little of the most current gossip and news. About a fourth of the entire congregation was made up of Beasleys.

ooooo◆ooooo

The second meeting of the Church Board of Trustees didn't go any better than the first. The divide between Trustees who wanted an addition and those who didn't was beginning to solidify. Of the six church officials, John Lewis and Jake Barnes were the most solid proponents of a new addition. Melvin Beasley was strongly opposed while Becca Switzer, Haywood Shedd, and Dave Filson seemed to be leaning towards the construction but were uncommitted outwardly. Reverend Miller made it clear that he wouldn't be involved and would support whatever the trustees decided.

"We have to keep up with the times, or everything is going to pass us by," said Jake Barnes at the beginning of the second meeting.

Melvin Beasley responded with, "I'm surprised that you think that 'keeping up with the times' is doing whatever the Baptists do."

"Awe, come on, Melvin, this has nothing to do with the Baptists. It is more about what they've already done and how it's affecting our numbers. Surely we don't want our church to dry up and disappear," responded John Lewis.

"There's nothing wrong with what we've always done, John," added Beasley. "These trends and fads come and go."

"Come on, Melvin," Barnes insisted, "losing our congregation has nothing to do with fads."

"Losing our congregation has nothing to do with nothing. The word of the Lord is clear on this. 'For where two or three have gathered together in my name, I am there in their midst.'"

"Yes, Melvin, right, of course, but listen," interjected John Lewis, "surly you see that having a more updated facility will make things nicer for all of us."

Melvin replied firmly, "And the scriptures are clear on this too, 'Not that I speak in respect of want: for I have learned, in whatsoever state I am, therewith to be content.'"

Dialogue of this type persisted for the duration of the meeting. There was no display of any loss of tempers, but it became clear as the meeting progressed that neither side in this debate was in the mood to yield. Melvin Beasley felt that the church should be a simple place to worship and should not have frills or unnecessary attractions. John Lewis and Jake Barnes believed that their church was in danger of losing so many members that it would eventually just dry up and have to close. It was clear from the questions and comments of the other three trustees that they were leaning towards the thoughts of Barnes and Lewis.

The six church leaders agreed to put off making a decision for a week so they could converse with other members of the congregation to determine what they were thinking. Melvin Beasley left the meeting with this parting shot, "I'll tell you one thing; if the final decision is to go ahead with this addition thing, the whole Beasley family is going to be more than just a little upset."

ooooo◆ooooo

John Lewis and Jake Barnes were making the rounds and calling on a few church members to survey them for their views concerning the dilemma of the church addition.

The two men decided to make their first stop at the farm of Peachy Cornett and his wife Eva. The two men were unsure how the couple would feel about the addition; in order to make room for the building, some trees had to be removed from an old fence row, and everyone knew how strongly Peachy and Eva felt about the preservation of trees. It was a beautiful sunshiny Saturday morning when they reached the long gravel driveway leading to the Cornett's. They reasoned that they would surely find the two together somewhere on the farm.

Peachy was in his mid forties when he met the slightly older widow, Eva Patterson. Theirs was a unique but perfect match. Peachy was the ultimate woodsman, and Eva was the dedicated scientist.

During his lifetime, Peachy spent more time in the woods hunting, trapping and foraging than most people spend in their living-rooms. He was somewhat limited in his formal education, but he knew all of the tricks of the forest. A few years earlier he had borrowed all the money he could and bought the Wilson Wright farm that joined the back of his place. The Wright place consisted of over two hundred acres of old-growth timber, and almost all of the acreage had never been logged. Peachy owned one of only five virgin forests in Kentucky.

Eva, on the other hand, had obtained a PHD in biology and was employed by the State University as a Research Biologist. She specialized in the study of indigenous and untouched forestland, and without really knowing Peachy, she began a serious study of his woods. She had received his permission to visit the place when she first moved into the area, but they had remained strangers to each other until they met one day in the middle of his woodlands.

They were immediately attracted to each other: both were impressed with what the other knew.

Their attraction to each other began on the day of their first meeting in the deep woods. They shared their knowledge of the forest and began to study the great woods together. The skilled woodsman and the educated biologist developed intense respect for the magnitude of the other's level of knowledge. When she began to see that beneath Peachy's huge six foot five frame was a kind and generous man, and when he realized that hidden behind Eva's crisp academic exterior was a gentle and loving lady, things changed for the both of them. The two fell hopelessly in love.

The newlyweds were sitting on their front porch when they saw Lewis's pickup coming up the long drive. Peachy jumped up and walked out and across the yard to the gravel turn-around place. He was waiting on the men when they got out of the truck.

When the two older men approached, Peachy did a little shadow boxing act, got a serious and menacing look on his face, and then said, "I guess you two came here to try to whup me for something I did or didn't do, huh?"

Jake Barnes laughed and answered with, "If we'd come to 'whup' you, we would have brought more people."

When the three men stopped laughing, Peachy Cornett invited the men up to sit on the front porch.

While they were walking, Peachy asked, "What's up? What brings you two here, church stuff?"

"We need to get your thoughts on the wisdom of the new addition," John Lewis said.

"Well, that's good, but first come up here, sit down, and let's visit for a minute," said Peachy.

When the trio reached the porch, Eva was standing waiting for them. After cordial greetings and gentle hugs, Eva suggested that the men might like some coffee. All three answered, "Yes," and Eva went through the front door and into the house.

Peachy turned and, over his shoulder, he said to Eva, "We'll just shoot the breeze a little until you get back with the coffee, Evie. You need to be here for the church stuff."

The men sat in the rockers that lined Cornett's porch and started right in with some small-talk. It was the usual practice around that part of Kentucky to engage in some conversation about the condition of the crops, the weather, who was sick, how the high school teams were doing, and anything else of interest, before delving right into business matters.

"Son, you sure got this place looking good," said Jake Barnes.

The view from Peachy's porch was, without doubt,

striking. The old, two-story, frame house sat on a pinnacle overlooking the rolling hay fields, and the fescue grass was still showing enough green to stand out in the sunlight. The fence was all relatively new and void of weeds and saplings. No junk or trash could be seen.

"Yeah," said John Lewis, "this place looks good enough to be on a calendar."

Peachy laughed.

"It wasn't always this way was it, Peachy?" asked John.

Peachy Cornett grew up on the place with his older brother, Samuel "Shorty" Cornett, and his sister, Dorothy. Their father, Walt, was a hard worker and a good man, but he was always buying old and overused equipment. When the stuff went kaput, he left it right where it was. The old farm became scattered with broken down junk and debris. In those days, the vista from the porch looked more like a junkyard than a cattle and tobacco farm.

When Walt Cornett passed, both Shorty and Dorothy had already moved off the place. Peachy bought the farm from his brother and sister and began the slow job of fixing up the place. Load after load of inoperative and broken equipment was hauled to Lexington Scrap Iron, new fence was built, and old fence repaired; barns and outbuildings rebuilt, and the old house was fixed up, fancied up, and modernized.

When Eva arrived with the coffee and sat with the men, the conversation drifted to her work, the woods, and the demise of the ash trees. Then of course there were some teasing questions about how she could survive having to put up with Peachy Cornett.

Peachy himself redirected the conversation when he asked, "All right, what's going on with the addition proposal?"

"We need to know what the membership thinks about it; what you two think about it," said John Lewis.

"Well, I haven't thought much about it, but of course I'm aware that there's the Beasley thing," said Peachy.

"Right, some of us are all for it, and some of us are not. Melvin Beasley is absolutely not for it, and I guess that means the entire Beasley outfit is opposed," said Jake Barnes.

"What's he saying?" asked Peachy Cornett.

"Melvin believes that anything that creates more

activities and events will be a disruption to our simple, community lifestyle," John Lewis said.

"Well, I guess he's got his point, but it seems to me that we'd be better off if we could offer a little more," said Peachy, and Eva nodded in agreement. "Can we afford it?"

"I don't think the money will be a problem," said John Lewis. "We'll have enough pledged to go along with what we already have to handle it."

"Is anybody else opposed to it?"

"Not really. Not that we know of, just the Beasleys."

"What about those trees?" Eva asked. "Somebody said they'd have to be cut."

"Yeah, unfortunately that's the only direction we can go with it," said John Lewis. "We've been wondering, and a little worried, about how you'd see that."

Peachy looked to Eva and waited for her judgment and reply. The lady frowned at first, then smiled and said, "Well, they're just old locust and hackberry fence-row trees, but they do look nice. They'll make a lot of nice firewood for somebody. If they gotta go, they gotta go"

Peachy shook his head "yes," looked around, took his hat off, and put his hands to his head. It was common knowledge, and sometimes joked about, that when Peachy Cornett began to rub his hair with both hands, he was thinking hard and about to make one final statement. And rubbing his head is exactly what he did right before he said, "Look, seems to me like we have to have it, or we are going to get left behind for sure."

"That's the way we see it, Peachy, but I'm afraid we're going to lose the whole Beasley outfit if we vote to go ahead with it."

"What do you mean lose them?"

"They might just up and leave the whole church."

"Lot of good an addition would do us then, huh?" said Peachy.

ooooo ◆ ooooo

The second meeting of the Board of Trustees went no better than the first. Melvin Beasley was adamant in his opposition to an addition. The meeting started pleasantly enough, but as the exchange of ideas and opinions progressed, and each side of the argument began to dig in, the situation began to get somewhat tense. John Lewis could see that the discussion had reached a dead end, and he made the suggestion that they call a third meeting, invite the entire church membership, and let a vote decide. The Board all agreed, and the second meeting was over.

On his way out, Melvin Beasley said, "This vote thing sure better go the right way."

The church controversy became the hot topic of interest around Mt. Zion. Wherever two or more people met, the subject came up. Members of the congregation expressed their concerns and voting intensions, and the rest of the community buzzed with speculations. The little community was united in its attention.

The Friday before the vote found John Lewis, Ernie Stone, and Peachy Cornett helping Shorty Cornett in his stripping room. The men were working at removing the leaves from the stalks, and the conversation naturally turned to the church and the controversy created by the prospects of an addition.

"How's the vote going to go tonight," asked Peachy Cornett.

John Lewis answered with, "My guess is that the Beasleys will all vote 'no', and the rest of us will vote 'yes.'"

"How will that count go?" asked Peachy.

"A lot depends on who all shows up."

"You can bet every single Beasley will be there."

"What about everybody else? I know Eva and I are going, and everybody I've talked to says they're going," said Peachy Cornett.

"I think most everybody will be there," said Ernie Stone. "What about you Shorty?"

"Oh yeah, we'll be there. Wouldn't miss it for the world."

After a little teasing about what it was taking to get everyone in church at the same time, the conversation turned serious.

"You know what's going to happen if the addition plan passes. The Beasleys will leave the church," said Shorty Cornett.

"Probably," said Peachy.

"Churches split all the time, but I really don't think our little congregation could stand it," said Ernie Stone.

"Do you really think Melvin would pull the whole outfit out?"

"I do."

"I'm not so sure. The Beasleys have been members since the beginning of time. They think it's their church," said John Lewis.

"If it passes, he's going to be mad. No telling what he'll do."

"Maybe we should forget the whole idea and vote against it," said Peachy.

"That doesn't seem right, does it?"

"Not really, but I don't want to lose the church."

And that's the way it went for most of the afternoon. For every question, there were two answers. The men were considered to be pillars of the little community and certainly of the church. Their influence would be felt, and their judgment respected. There just didn't appear to be a right answer.

ooooo ◆ ooooo

The third meeting at the Mt. Zion First Christian Church was scheduled for 7:00 PM that Friday night, but folks began to show up much earlier. They began filing into the meeting room shortly after 6:30, and by 6:45 the place was getting rather crowded. The church members were standing around talking in low murmurs. It was almost 7 o'clock before the Beasley's showed up, and when they did, it was apparent that every single Beasley would be there to vote. Melvin Beasley was determined.

John Lewis immediately saw that meeting room was too small to accommodate the entire congregation, and he suggested that they all move to the sanctuary. As the church members were changing rooms, people were counting heads and whispering about just how many Beasley's there were. The relaxed demeanor of the crowd changed abruptly and became a little tense: there was no laughing and very few smiles.

John Lewis gave a short speech to make sure that there would be no misunderstandings about the purpose of the meeting and vote. The Trustees had determined earlier that the best way to poll the congregation was with a printed ballot. The ballots were handed out, and a handful of pencils were passed around as well. When everyone had voted, Melvin Beasley, Ernie Stone, and Reverend Miller gathered up the ballots and took them to the table to be counted.

When the men finish tabulating the votes, John Lewis announced to the group that the majority had voted in favor of building a new room addition. There was a rush of loud talking, and then the crowd stood, talked some more, and began to file out of the church. John Lewis watched Melvin Beasley to gauge his reaction. Beasley didn't say a word. He was white faced and grim as he stood and walked out of the church. His extended family followed him

Ernie Stone, Harold Browning, and John Lewis were among the last to leave the church. They met on the steps to chat.

"It's not going to be good," offered Harold Browning.

"No, I think he'll leave," said Ernie.

"Yeah, I'd say that's what's going to happen," said John Lewis. "Our little church is going to get smaller."

ooooo◆ooooo

John Lewis didn't sleep well the night of the vote. He tossed and turned and wondered if he had done the right thing by pushing on with the vote. He was second guessing himself, and he got up long before daylight. Lewis had plans to meet Jake Barnes at his place at 9:00AM that morning to help with a plumbing job. For John, it seemed like forever before it was time to leave.

A very tired John Lewis drove down his long driveway and turned towards Mt. Zion when he reached the highway. Jake's place was on the other side of the little town, and John Lewis had enough time to stop in at McBride's store and talk to McBride or anyone else who had stopped in on their way to work.

John did not get out at the store. When he pulled into the gravel parking spot, he was confused by what he saw just down the road. There were several trucks, a tractor, and what looked like a wagon along the side of the Christian church. John pulled back out onto the highway and headed straight to his church to see what was going on.

John Lewis was shocked to see Melvin Beasley and a whole crew of his family with chain saws, log chains, and a tractor: they were cutting down the trees in the fencerow.

Lewis got out of his truck and walked up the slight incline towards the men. When Melvin Beasley saw him approaching, he waved for john to come up to where he was standing. Then he shouted, "You'd better get up here and help. If we've got to get rid of these trees before we build that new room, we'd better go on and get started!"

John Lewis could not help himself. He broke out in a smile.

Georgette

There wasn't much to the town of Mt. Zion, Kentucky. McBride's Grocery, two churches, Riggs's Service Station, a radiator shop, and four side streets made up the quaint place. The stores and four or five houses were situated along the highway that ran through the tiny community, and on each side of the highway there were a couple of side streets with ten to twelve houses each. Mt. Zion was an uncomplicated and quiet little settlement.

Franklin Rudd lived on one of the two side streets of Mt. Zion with his mother and two younger sisters. His father was long gone and had not been heard from for years. Franklin was entering his 15th year but was responsible and mature beyond his years: he had been thrust into the role of babysitter and guardian to his younger sisters at a very early age.

There wasn't much traffic on the back streets of Mt. Zion, and the pavement provided the perfect playground for Franklin and the other kids of the community. Most every summer evening, the streets would host a game of hide and seek, kick the can, devil on the sidewalk, or anything else that young imaginations could dream up. Artie Shedd, Franklin, and their sisters made up the core of youngsters on one side of the highway, while the Switzer brothers and Woody Ziegler made up the contingent from the other side. Great games were sure to happen when everyone was around, but when a few were away visiting, sick, or working late in the hay or tobacco fields, the games became less keen.

The number of available participants was boosted significantly when Georgette Parks and her sisters showed up. She was the oldest of three skinny, long-legged sisters who lived in a neighboring county but frequently visited her grandparents. The elderly couple lived in a large white two-story house directly across the street from Franklin, and although they lived alone, there was always a lot of comings and goings around their house. The Parks girls sometimes arrived for visits on winter weekends, but they became semi-permanent residents of the neighborhood during the summer months.

When Georgette and her sisters were in town, they were welcomed as beneficial additions to the playground scene. When added to the Switzers, Shedds, and Rudds, the girls provided the needed numbers for a game of kick-ball or even baseball. In the early days of his youth, Franklin Rudd's perception of Georgette was exactly like that of any other boy or girl living in the area: she was there, she joined in all of the games and carryings-on, and that was that. They were just a bunch of kids hanging out together, gabbing, playing ball, and having what can only be described as good, clean fun.

ooooo◆ooooo

The Parks girls didn't make the visit to their grandparents' house from Christmas until June of that year. Georgette's absence wasn't noticed that winter: from late autumn until spring, 1967 had been cold and bitter, and there was very little outdoor play going on. But when Georgette again showed up on a warm day in May, holy smokes did Franklin ever notice. The young man had walked out onto his front porch, looked across the street, and there she was getting out of her mother's car. *Oh-my-gosh something was way different!* Georgette was still long-legged, but she was long-legged and very much not skinny. She had shape! She had a figure. And her hair was up. Georgette was a beauty, and Franklin began to behave like he knew that life in the neighborhood was going to unfold in a much different way.

The young man went back into his house. He brushed his teeth and combed his hair before he went back onto the porch and headed across the street. Throughout the neighborhood, the beckoning signal of salutation had always been a short shrill whip-poor-will like whistle, and when Franklin got to the Park's front yard, he sounded the piercing call. In a few seconds, Georgette came bounding down her front steps, skipped over to the boy smiling, lightly punched him on the shoulder, and asked something like ten straight questions about his winter, everybody else, and everything else. Despite the fact that she was a year older and now came packaged in this new and extraordinary way, she was somehow the same old Georgette. She had her same self assuredness and relaxing ways, but there was little doubt that Franklin was seeing her in a much different light.

From that moment on, there was a power, an unexplainable gravity-like force, that pulled Franklin in the direction of Georgette. He began to spend increasingly more and more time somewhere around the young lady. She didn't object to his presence, and that just cranked up the magnetic force for Franklin.

Georgette was beginning to take over most of Franklin's thoughts. The young lady was becoming central to everything in his young life. They would take walks together and were much less interested in playing with the other kids. On one of their long walks, Franklin mustered up the courage to reach down and take her hand in his. His heart was racing, and Franklin half expected rejection, a push, or even a slap, but she just took his hand, and they walked on half swinging their arms. After that, they could be seen walking down the street hand in hand; laughing and acting silly while they bumped hips trying to knock each other off balance. Holding hands is what they did.

Franklin Rudd and Georgette Parks held hands, kissed, promised to love one another forever, laughed, loved, and lived in bliss for the rest of the summer. Their days overflowed with a grand sweetness. Young love was theirs.

∞∞∞∞◆∞∞∞∞

There was one event that was celebrated by all of the boys living around Mt. Zion, and that was when a mid-summer storm poured enough rain into Rock Creek and Sandy Fork to get them running full. The hot days of June and early July reduced the streams to just a trickle, the waters became slack and sat in pools, and the fish quit biting. When the rains poured in and got the creeks flowing hard, the fish swam upstream to feed. The creeks had several small dams that had been built over the years to hold water for livestock, and when the red-eye, blue gill, and small-mouth bass got to the dams, they could go no further. The fish would amass there and feed with gusto on whatever washed over the dams or was cast in by fishermen. Even the most unlucky fisherman could catch plenty in no time.

Whenever the young men heard that the water was up, they didn't hesitate to dig some worms, get their poles, and head straight to the creeks. Their fathers, uncles, and grandfathers had done the same thing. It didn't happen often, and it wasn't to be missed.

Thunderstorms and torrential rain struck the county during the night. It was mid July, and the men were up early to check their crops, outbuildings, and fences to see if there was damage from the deluge and wind. It was not uncommon for them to stop in at McBride's store during the mornings, and certainly this morning was not an exception: they would want to know how their neighbors had fared. It was here that they got the word from Ernie Stone that the creeks were running hard and rising. That knowledge passed quickly to the boys.

When Woody Ziegler heard from his uncle that the creeks were up, he headed straight to the Switzers. He found Philip and Eddie Switzer in the old smokehouse behind their house where they were gathering up their fishing poles. The Switzer's obviously had already heard.

"Let's go get Franklin and Artie, dig some worms, and hit the big dam first," said Phillip Switzer.

"Yeah, let's go," replied Woody. "But I have to stop by and get my stuff. Let's go."

The threesome half walked and half ran down their street, across the highway, and up the cross street to Artie Shedd's home. When they shouted and whistled, Artie came out, saw his friends with their fishing poles, and without saying a word, turned and went back in to get his. The last stop for the young fishermen was Franklin Rudd's, and they found their friend sitting on his front porch.

"Let's go, Frankie," Artie half shouted. "The creeks are up."

"Well, I, ugh…," Franklin started to stammer. "I don't think I'll go this morning."

"You've got to be kidding. What's wrong?" Woody asked.

"Nothing really. I, ugh, I've got something else I have to do. You all go on. Maybe I can catch up with you later," said Franklin.

The boys looked at each other, shrugged, nodded, and turned to go. It was then that Artie looked across

the street and noticed Georgette emerging from her front door. Artie stopped abruptly and turned around and faced Franklin with a wide eyed look of disbelief. He said nothing. Of course the other boys saw Georgette too, and it became clear to each of them that Franklin had his priorities messed up.

As they hustled off to the creeks, not a word was said for the longest time. Then the silence was broken when Artie Shedd blurted out, "He's crazy, do you believe that?"

The other boys all laughed, and they picked up their pace.

∞∞∞∞◆∞∞∞∞

When the summer ended and school restarted, Georgette's visits to the neighborhood became less frequent. Franklin's efforts advanced into writing letters, crafting and mailing semi-plagiarized poetry, and initiating lengthy telephone calls. Georgette responded with equal enthusiasm. The bright light of love didn't flicker or dim a bit.

Franklin was resolute in his determination to prove to Georgette that his love was true and undying. It seemed that he would do anything for the young lady. And in his effort to insure that her love for him was equal to his for her, he was relentless in his efforts to demonstrate all of his extraordinary abilities. And then out of the blue, a great chance to prove both ability and love presented itself.

Georgette was baffled by her new biology teacher's project assignment. She was given the choice of putting together either a leaf or an insect/bug collection, and she knew nothing about leaves or bugs. Georgette had always been an excellent student, but this leaf/bug thing was daunting to her. She worried until she worked herself up into an awful state. In her fear, Georgette asked Franklin if maybe he could help. When she told the young man what the two choices were, Franklin immediately became the world's foremost expert on bugs. He told her not to worry; he would not only help her, but he would, in fact, put together a bug display for her. It turns out that in the end this wasn't necessarily a real swift move on his part.

Franklin Rudd promised Georgette that he would have her bug collection completed for her by the time she next visited her grandfather. At that moment, the boy was sure that Georgette believed he was the greatest, the smartest, and the most talented guy in the entire world. Indeed, right then she did know exactly why she was so much in love with Franklin.

And of course, he was feeling like a king and walking around with a skip in his step and his chest puffed out.

One thing that made the bug display endeavor so interesting was the fact that academic pursuit had certainly never been Franklin's strong suit. Some of his teachers might have gone so far as to say that the boy was probably one of the least motivated students in the history of Rock Creek School. But that didn't faze Franklin: he threw himself into the insect/bug project like he was the ultimate biologist. If he had studied half as hard as he worked at Georgette's science project, he would have surely been the most accomplished student ever. But that didn't slow him down one whit; he was consumed with his work on the bug project. He was resolute in his effort to impress Georgette.

To Franklin, the plan seemed simple enough. Georgette was to bring him a felt covered piece of heavy poster board. Mr. Ziegler told Franklin that he would make an extra nice frame for it in his wood-working shop, and his sister agreed to print the paper labels for each example in her beautiful handwriting. Franklin would catch the bugs, permanently slow them down by dropping them into a jar with a cotton ball soaked in carbon tetrachloride, and then make one trip to the library in Hawkinsville and look up their scientific names. Mounting them with those tiny straight pins would be a snap.

By no means was Franklin Rudd an inside-the-house sort of young man. He did in fact know quite a bit about trees, leaves, bugs, and things related to the outdoors. Georgette had told Franklin that a minimum of thirty varieties were required, and he immediately set out to gather them up. The young man started poking around the trees and weeds. He sneaked about lifting rocks and garbage can lids. He looked everywhere. June bugs, grasshoppers, pinching bugs, lightning bugs, lady bugs, crickets, a super praying mantis, and eighteen others accounted for the twenty-six varieties that he was able to catch and name. Franklin found and caught several others that he knew nothing about, but he could not, to save his life, identify a single additional living bug-like creature. His knowledge of insects ended at the number twenty-six. The undertaking wasn't turning out exactly as he had planned.

Like all the boys of that age, Franklin was naturally rather quick on his feet and sometimes even given to some small degree of deviousness. This combination led Franklin to thoughts of how he might utilize the extra bugs he had collected but couldn't identify. He didn't have to think too long. In less than one minute, Franklin realized how easy it would be just dream up some cool sounding name for each and then simply add them to the collection. Of course, that's exactly what he determined he would do. Franklin was absolutely sure that neither Georgette nor her teacher would ever know the difference. All that was needed was a little nerve.

Franklin opted to go the library at his very first opportunity. His mission was to look in those big technical books to get new scientific names. He would merely take parts of the Latin words from several living creatures and mix them around to come up with his own spanky-new scientific names. Franklin's sister, Dava, offered her help, and with the advantage of her creativity, he ended up with exciting examples. He had a Long Nosed Beetle (*Coleoptera Cerambycidae*), a Silver Grass Crawler (*Caeliferce Pneumoroidea*), and two other similarly named beauties. This piece of the entire project was the fun part. There he was with his sister in the Hawkinsville Library, pouring over the books, laughing, cutting up, and getting mean looks from the librarians for making too much noise.

Franklin put the whole thing together, and it was good. He thought it was spectacular. His sister thought it was beautiful and that it looked quite professional. Georgette was so excited when Franklin handed it to her on her next visit to the neighborhood. She smiled first, and then she started clapping her hands and jumping up and down. Then Franklin and Georgette both burst out laughing. Franklin Rudd was bursting with pride.

For the next week or so, Franklin called Georgette every afternoon after school, and it was never more than a few seconds before he asked if the bug project had been graded. She was so impressed with his concern. She believed his impatience resulted from his sincere concern about her grades and her educational wellbeing. Of course, "wellbeing" was at the top of his list of concerns, but it was his own wellbeing: Franklin knew that his life of bliss would be wrecked if the bug scam were detected.

Finally Georgette called Franklin to tell him that she had finally received the grade, and that it was an A+. The young man was relieved beyond belief. "*I pulled it off,*" he thought. "*Success!*"

But wait, there was more, and the news was not all that exciting. The science teacher was so impressed with the bug project that she encouraged Georgette to enter it into the six-county science fair, and Georgette had enthusiastically agreed. There was nothing Franklin could do but fake some wholehearted congratulations. Experts, real experts, would be examining it this time, and his hoax would be revealed. Franklin began to believe that he was doomed. At that moment, if the young man could have gotten his hands on that insect display, it would have disappeared forever!

Georgette did in fact enter the contest, and once again, Franklin had to endure the long wait. The science fair event didn't take place for another three weeks, so he had a little time to try a desperation move: he suggested to Georgette that he should make a small adjustment to the display and that she should bring it to him so he could "doll it up" a little for the great event. She refused and said she liked it just like it was, so the wait was on.

The Saturday of the science fair was not a pleasant day for Franklin. It had stormed the night before, and once again, Franklin couldn't join his friends in fishing the creeks. He had to stick around the phone and wait to hear the news from Georgette. He kept telling himself that by some miracle the deception wouldn't be discovered, and the episode would end well, but that little trick of self deception really didn't work. He could think of nothing but Georgette, and he kept seeing an image of her face when it was revealed that her entry was a hoax. Franklin could vision her, and what it was going to feel like for her when she was accused of having cheated. She was to be humiliated, and a lot of unpleasant stuff was going to come Franklin's way. It was not a fun day for the young man.

It was close to noon when Georgette called. Franklin picked up the phone, and in a voice that was as sweet as he could make it, he spoke calmly into the receiver. "Hello," he mellowed.

The first clue that things hadn't gone well for Georgette could be found in her first words. "I hope you drop dead!" she half shouted.

Franklin was reasonably sure he could weasel out of his mess, and he said in the most surprised sounding voice he could muster, "Well, what are you…"

"Don't 'well what' me. How could you? Don't act like you don't know what you did," said Georgette.

"I was trying to….," Franklin said before being interrupted in mid sentence again.

"I don't want to hear it. I don't want to hear you."

"Georgette….," Franklin again tried to speak.

"I hope I never see you again!" And with that, she hung up.

ooooo ◆ ooooo

Franklin Rudd sat perfectly still for two or three minutes. He hadn't expected the outcome to be quite that dramatic. It took the young man a little time for the realization to sink in that he wasn't going to talk his way out of the mess he'd made. But, sink in it did, and as he dealt with the terrible understanding that his sweet life with Georgette was over, he was overcome with remorse. The pain and anguish were severe for seven or eight minutes. It was at that time that he heard Artie, Woody, and Eddie jabbering as they made their way back to the fishing holes. Franklin realized at once that his friends had been home for lunch and were going back to fish some more. Franklin Rudd grabbed his fishing pole and bounded out the front door and down the steps. When he hit the front yard, he shouted in a voice the whole neighborhood could hear, "Hey, wait for me!"

CPSIA information can be obtained
at www.ICGtesting.com
Printed in the USA
FFOW04n1509250715
15356FF